THE KISS OF
THE DRAGON
LADY

H.L. Slater

For Shari

CHAPTER ONE

Frank Pierce leaned back in his chair and propped his feet up on the desk. He had picked up the swivel chair and oak desk for thirty dollars for both in the basement of a secondhand furniture store on Mission Street. Used and discarded like the rest of the furniture in the sparse office —including a comfortable, if worn, Moroccan leather couch on which he had spent several nights sleeping off a hangover after his divorce—the desk and chair suited him, for Pierce felt used up, worn out, and discarded.

The telephone on the desk had rung only once in over a week. Pierce couldn't remember if he had paid the bill. He picked up the receiver just to check if the phone was working, heard a dial tone, and replaced the handset back on its hook. He considered getting one of those new phones with buttons, maybe in color, then dismissed the idea as frivolous. He had more immediate matters to think about.

At ten o'clock that night, he would be sitting in the back of a Ford Econoline and watching the freight dock in the rear of Williams & Chow Import-Export Co., Ltd. Marcus Williams himself had called and asked Pierce to investigate the disappearance of crates of merchandise from his waterfront warehouse, shortages that went beyond occasional small-time pilfering.

At Williams's insistence, Pierce drove down the peninsula to Williams's home in Los Altos Hills for a meeting with his prospective client. He found Williams's stately, two-story colonial without too much difficulty, only making a single wrong turn along the narrow lanes leading to the top of the hill overlooking the surrounding countryside. At the end of a long drive, he parked in the circular driveway in front of four white columns rising to a balcony at the roof above the entrance.

An Asian butler met Pierce at the door.

"You come please. Mister Williams waiting. You come," the butler said.

From the butler's accent, Pierce figured that the stocky, strongly built man was more than likely born in China and probably spoke Cantonese, which Pierce understood a little from working the streets of Chinatown, although the words he knew were not often heard in the upper reaches of society.

The butler led Pierce across the white marble floor of the foyer to heavy sliding doors. The butler knocked lightly before sliding the doors open and motioning Pierce to enter the room. Once inside, the doors closed silently behind Pierce.

"Mr. Pierce, please come in," Marcus Williams said.

Williams sat in a leather wingback chair near a large fireplace in which a small fire was burning although the afternoon was warm. He was dressed in brown slacks, a white dress shirt, and a gray cardigan. He had a green and blue plaid blanket draped across his lap.

"Please sit here near me," Williams said gesturing to a

chair, a duplicate of the one in which he was sitting.

Pierce looked around the wood paneled room which somehow reminded him of a library except there were neither shelves nor books in evidence.

Pierce sat down.

"Can I get you something to drink, Mr. Pierce?"

"I'm okay, thanks."

Pierce liked to keep his wits about him when dealing with people strange to him, especially clients, and in his experience, most clients were strange and usually had something to hide.

"I like to have a glass of sherry in the afternoon. Are you sure I can't offer you anything? Coffee, perhaps?" Williams asked.

"Well, if it's no trouble, coffee would be fine."

Williams reached to the small table beside his chair and pushed a button hidden underneath. No sooner had he done that when the butler appeared in the doorway.

"Yes, sir?" the butler said.

"I'd like my usual sherry, and Mr. Pierce would like—," he said and looked to Pierce and continued, "How do you like your coffee, Mr. Pierce?"

"Black," Pierce answered.

"And a black coffee for our guest, Yan-ling."

"Yes, sir," the butler said and left the room as quietly as he had entered.

"Shall we get down to business, Mr. Williams? I don't think you invited me down here for afternoon tea," Pierce said.

"Right you are, Mr. Pierce. But let's wait a moment before we begin, shall we?"

Right on cue the butler returned with a silver tray on which a glass of sherry and a cup of coffee sat. He put the sherry down on the table next to Williams, and the cup of coffee on a small table next to Pierce, and left the room.

Williams took a sip from his glass and settled back in his chair. "What do you know about Chinese artifacts, Mr. Pierce?"

"Not much beyond the usual phony junk you see in Chinatown."

"Quite right. I, or I should say my partner, Dr. Chow and I, import most of the things, or junk as you say, that one sees in the shops along Grant Avenue."

Williams took another sip from his glass and continued, "However once in a while, Dr. Chow finds something unusual and sends it to me with our regular shipments here in San Francisco."

"Your partner, Dr. Chow, is in China then?"

"Yes, he lives in Hong Kong."

Williams went on, "Lately however, our shipments, our merchandise, have come up short."

"And you suspect your partner for these..."

"Oh, no, no, Dr. Chow and I are more than business partners. We are best, let us say more than best, friends."

"So then you don't suspect your partner?" Pierce asked.

"Absolutely not. I've known Paul since the beginning of the war. We served in China together. When you get to know someone like that, you learn to trust him with your life."

"Paul? That's a rather unusual name for a person from China," Pierce said.

"Paul is his Christian name. True, he was born in China, but he was raised in a well-to-do Catholic family in Canton and educated at a parish school."

Pierce took a sip of his coffee.

"I see," he said.

The Kiss of the Dragon Lady

"No, I don't think you do. Let me tell you about Paul Chow."

Williams, trying to get more comfortable, shifted his weight in his chair.

"When Japan invaded China in '37, Paul was a medical student in Shanghai. He dropped out of the university and joined China's Army to attend wounded Chinese soldiers, who were defending the city against the Japanese.

"After the city fell, Paul made his way to Kunming, where the Chinese Air Force was headquartered, and started working as a doctor at the base's infirmary."

Williams paused and shifted in his chair once again before taking another sip of his sherry.

"I thought you said Chow dropped out of medical school before earning his degree," Pierce said.

Williams smiled.

"That's true enough. He lied about his lack of credentials, saying that they were destroyed when the university was bombed by the Japanese. But it didn't matter in any event. The Chinese were desperate for anyone who had skills to help in the war effort, and Paul was a competent surgeon having learned on the job, so to speak, in Shanghai."

"And that's where you met Chow?"

"Yes, China's warlord, Chiang Kai-shek, pleaded with America for help after being deserted by the Soviets. I was an Army Air Corps pilot before the war, so when President Roosevelt created the First American Volunteer Group, I signed up," Williams said.

"You were in the Flying Tigers?"

"Yes," Williams said with pride.

Williams took another sip from his glass of sherry, and again shifted in his chair.

"Where was I? Oh, yes. We were shipped out to Rangoon in the summer of '41 for training. I'd like to tell you that we were crackerjack plane jockeys, but nothing could be further from the truth. Although we were recruited from the Navy, Marines, and the Air Corps, a few of the boys had never even flown a plane. I had been a bomber pilot, so P-40 fighter tactics were all new to me. After training, we were sent to Kunming, but we didn't fly our first mission until twelve days after Pearl Harbor."

"And your partner, Paul Chow, how did you meet?" Pierce asked.

Williams reflected for a moment.

"Well, not as you might think. I was nervous before our first mission."

Williams paused.

"That's normal, I'd say," Pierce said.

"As you might guess, we were all mad as hell about Pearl Harbor and wanted revenge against the Japs as soon as possible. I was 'young and dumb' as the saying goes, but even so at twenty-five, I was thought of as an old man."

"So, you were the 'old man.'"

"Oh, good heavens, no. General Chennault was *the* 'old man.' That was his nickname. That's what everyone called him. But some of the boys, and that's all they were then, weren't old enough to buy a beer back in the States. But they were about to become men well beyond their years."

Pierce said nothing and took a sip of his coffee, which had now grown cold, as he waited for Williams to continue.

Williams noticed the slight grimace on Pierce's face as Pierce tasted the cold coffee and reached again for the button under the table.

The Kiss of the Dragon Lady

"Here, let's freshen that up for you," Williams said.

He had barely finished speaking when Yan-ling appeared at Pierce's side. The butler picked up the cold coffee and replaced it with a fresh cup before vanishing.

"You were saying?" Pierce said.

Williams sat deep in thought for a few minutes before answering.

"That day, I remember it was a Saturday, twelve days after Pearl Harbor. Like I said, I was nervous. We all were. None of us had seen real combat before. But we were ready to fight. Then the word came down. We scrambled to intercept Jap bombers over Kunming. The Jap fighters were quick and nimble so we couldn't engage them in a turning dogfight, but our P-40's had more firepower and could dive faster. We used that to our advantage by climbing above the enemy, then diving and slashing at their aircraft, and then diving away to set up another attack. That first day we shot down ten Jap bombers, losing only one of our Warhawks.

"All through the attack, the adrenaline was pumping hard through my body. But when it was over, and we were returning to the airfield, I felt woozy. I looked down and saw my lap and left leg covered in blood. I had never felt a thing during the fight, but now my leg was on fire, and I was fighting to keep awake. I remember coming in sight of the airfield and lining up for the landing. I don't know how I ever landed that plane, but the next thing I remember is waking up to the face of a Chinese doctor standing over me. 'Welcome back, I'm Doctor Chow,' he said.

"So you see, I had been shot up pretty badly. Paul Chow operated on me and saved my leg..., and my life."

CHAPTER TWO

Pierce looked at his watch: 4:31 a.m. Five minutes had passed since he last checked. The fog had settled in around two o'clock, dropping the temperature inside the van from uncomfortable to downright miserable. He made a mental note to dress warmer if this stakeout lasted past this first night.

He sat in a portable beach chair with his camera in the rear of the van. He had a clear shot of the loading dock through the van's rear windows, and a nearby streetlight gave enough light to capture a decent photograph with high-speed black and white film. But the fog had grown thick, clinging to the van's windows and sending rivulets streaking down the glass, obscuring Pierce's view. He would have to reach out and wipe the condensation off the windows exposing his presence if anyone was watching.

Pierce was about to chance it when headlights flashed into the alley. A red Mustang convertible, its top up, slowly passed his vantage point and stopped at the loading dock. He released the camera's shutter. Perhaps he would get a clear shot of the license plate if he was lucky. The car, its motor running, waited for a few minutes before it continued on and turned left into the street at the far end of the alleyway. The Mustang wouldn't be hard to spot if he saw it again. He decided to wait it out. Maybe the Mustang would make another pass, and he didn't want to take a chance of being spotted.

Pierce had remembered to include a lawn chair in the van, but he cursed himself for not bringing blankets. The cold was making him sleepy. He fought to keep awake. He poured some coffee into the cup from his thermos. The coffee was still hot enough to ward off at least some of the chill. He checked his watch again. It was after five o'clock and soon the warehousemen would be coming to work, and he could go home and get a few hours of sleep before reporting back to Williams.

Rene crept into his thoughts. She always did when he got so tired that he could no longer keep the thought of her at bay. They were sitting on a blanket at Stinson Beach. The beach was not crowded, with only a few people braving the overcast sky attempting to coax the sun out of hiding by lying on brightly colored towels.

Farther down the beach, five or six hardy souls in wet suits were surfing the waves. Rene sat on the blanket in her black bikini, her shoulder-length chestnut hair wet from a quick swim in the icy ocean. She had always relished daring what others would not. She turned to look at him and gave a faint smile.

A bang on the side of the van woke Pierce with a start.

"Hey, I know you're in there. I kin see the steam on the windows," a man's voice shouted.

Pierce moved to the driver's seat and rolled down the window to see a swarthy, thickset man.

"Can't ya read the sign? I don't give a shit if ya sleep here, but ya gotta be outta here before five. Else I can't back the trucks up to the dock," the man said.

As a matter of fact, Pierce hadn't paid any attention to the sign figuring that he would be gone before anyone noticed him. He checked his watch: 6:45.

"Sorry, I'll move right away," he said and started the engine.

"Don't let me see ya around here again," the man yelled as Pierce drove away.

"Fuck," Pierce said out loud.

All he got for his sleepless night was a red convertible which may or may not have anything to do with anything, a stiff neck, and a pounding headache. His only consolation was that Williams was paying him two hundred dollars a day, plus expenses, a good week's pay in any other job.

He not only struck out his first night, but also was discovered to boot. Pierce decided he would call Williams after he got back to the office and see if Williams wanted him to continue with the surveillance.

Pierce drove up Twenty-fourth Street toward his office on the north side of the street between Noe and Castro and parked around the corner on Sanchez Street. The chill morning air felt good on his face as he walked the remaining two blocks. The office itself was on the second floor of a two-story building built shortly after San Francisco's 1906 Earthquake. O'Callaghan's Pub occupied the ground floor.

Several drivers, their delivery trucks double parked in the street, stood in front of the bar waiting for it to open. This ritual happened every morning except Sunday. On Sundays, most of the men waited until after their wives dragged them to morning mass before downing their first

The Kiss of the Dragon Lady

bracer to get them through the day.

As always, Michael O'Callaghan, Mickey O' to friend and foe alike, unlocked the pub door at seven o'clock on the nose. Any delay would call for loud protests from his jittery customers. The waiting men didn't have any time to waste. They had to get to their delivery routes.

Pierce followed the drivers into the bar. He waited until they threw back their shots of Jameson Irish Whiskey or the cheaper Old Crow. After the men had fortified themselves and filed out, Mickey scooped up the money they had left on the bar and rang it up on the register, most of it anyway. After all, a little off the top that the tax man didn't have to know about wasn't skin off anyone's nose. Stealing from friends and neighbors was a sin; cheating the tax man was a virtue.

O'Callaghan, a strongly built man with black wavy hair and bright blue eyes, put a shot glass on the bar in front of Pierce and filled it with Jameson. Pierce threw it down in a single gulp, put the glass back on the bar and nodded for Mickey to refill it.

"Tough night, Frank?" O'Callaghan asked.

"Yeah, freezing my ass off in a back alley off of Brannan."

"You should find yourself an easier line of work."

"I did, it didn't work out, remember."

Pierce paused and then continued, "Say, you ever heard of a bigwig named Williams, Marcus Williams?"

"Import-Export?"

"Yeah, that's the guy. What do you know about him?"

"You better not be fucking around with that guy if you're smart," O'Callaghan said.

"That's the first time you ever suggested that I'm smart. Who is this guy Williams?"

"Smart, you ain't. Williams's got friends downtown, and it's rumored he's connected."

"By connected, you mean the mob?"

"Hey, you didn't hear anything from me, but that's the rumor. Before I set myself up here, you know that I worked on the docks. Things would grow legs and walk away, know what I mean? The Customs guys would come around and ask questions. Williams would show up and everything would be copasetic, know what I mean?"

"Thanks for the tip," Pierce said, finished his whiskey, and got up from his barstool.

"Put it on the tab, okay?"

"Sure, you're good for it. And, Frank, be careful with that guy Williams."

Pierce started for the door.

"Wait a minute, Frank," O'Callaghan said. "If I remember rightly, Williams was a Police Commissioner when you were a cop."

Pierce stopped. "He was, huh? I don't remember who the hell was on the Commission. I never had anything to do with the Commission..., at least not until they fired me."

"I thought you quit," O'Callaghan said.

"I did," Pierce said and walked out of the bar.

CHAPTER THREE

Back in his office, Pierce woke on his leather couch to the ringing of his phone. At first, he didn't know where he was. He sat up and shook his head, quickly realizing that doing so was a mistake. He made his way to his desk and picked up the phone.

"Good morning, *Discreet Inquires*," he said into the handset.

"Good *afternoon*. Is this Mr. Pierce?" asked a woman at the other end of the line.

Afternoon?

"Yes, this is Frank Pierce."

"This is Susan Li. I'm Mr. Williams's Personal Assistant. Mr. Williams was expecting to hear from you this morning," the woman said.

Pierce's head was pounding, but his mind was clearing.

"Everything is going fine. I have been preparing a written report for Mr. Williams," he said.

"That will not be necessary. As a matter of fact, written reports are frowned upon by Mr. Williams. He insists on face-to-face progress reports. Is that understood?"

"Got it, nothing in writing."

"Good. It's one o'clock now. Mr. Williams expects to see you at his home at two," the woman said and hung up.

Pierce replaced the handset and checked his watch. He had just enough time to make it if he left right away. But first, he needed a couple of Alka-Seltzers to kill the hangover aggravated by his sleepless night. The two double shots of Jameson had nothing to do with his condition, he was sure.

After shaving and putting on a clean shirt, he pulled on his corduroy jacket and bounded down the stairs two treads at a time to the street. He hurried down Twenty-fourth, crossed the street, and walked up Noe two blocks to his apartment building where he rented a one bedroom. He had been lucky to find the apartment and even luckier to get a garage in the same building for only ten bucks extra a month.

Pierce backed his car, a British Green '64 Austin-Healey, out of the garage and onto the street. The car had cost him close to four grand when he bought it new, but it was worth it. He could afford it then. A seventeen-year veteran in the Police Department and passing the promotional exam for inspector, he felt the need to celebrate his anticipated advancement. That the expensive sports car would prove to aid in his demise didn't lessen his enthusiasm for the Healey. Maybe it had been a mistake to buy it, but what the fuck, he thought, that was all water under the bridge now.

He cut across town to Alemany Boulevard where he caught El Camino Real south to Los Altos Hills and took the Page Mill Road exit. This time he didn't make any wrong turns and found the driveway leading up the hill without difficulty. At the top of the driveway, he saw the Red Mustang convertible parked in front of the house. He took note of the license number and reminded himself to develop the film from the night before.

At the house, the butler opened the door even as Pierce approached. Yan-ling said nothing only nodded slightly in recognition and motioned Pierce to follow him again to the wood-paneled study. Once inside, he found Marcus Williams in the same chair with the same plaid blanket across his lap.

"Good afternoon, Mr. Williams," he said.

"I expected you this morning, Mr. Pierce. What do you have for me?" Williams asked.

Pierce ignored the brusqueness in Williams's tone. He told Williams what had occurred the night before including his run in with the big guy at the loading dock but leaving out the sighting of the Mustang. A little voice inside told him that this detail should be left unsaid at least for the time being.

"That would have been Guido Rossi, my dock foreman. I'm sorry he saw you. Be more careful in the future. He can get nasty if he gets riled up."

"Then you want me to continue the surveillance?"

"Of course. You didn't expect to find out anything in just one night, did you? That would've been highly unlikely."

Williams pressed the button under the table and the butler was at Pierce's side.

"Yan-ling, show Mr. Pierce out."

The butler led Pierce back into the foyer.

"You wait," Yan-ling said and disappeared into a nearby anteroom.

"Mr. Pierce, thank you for waiting."

Pierce looked up to the top of the spiral staircase

leading to the second floor. Descending the stairs was a tall, strikingly beautiful Eurasian woman. Standing almost six feet, she was nearly as tall as he. She was dressed in a dark blue business suit over a stiffly starched white blouse. She wore her black hair pulled up and held in place with silver combs. She had on large sunglasses with round lenses set in a thin wire frame. A Chinese Dragon set to strike, Pierce thought.

When the woman reached the bottom of the stairs, she held out her hand to Pierce.

"I'm Susan Li. We spoke on the phone."

Pierce took the woman's hand lightly.

"How do you do, Ms. Li," he said as he tried to detect her eyes behind the dark glasses.

"I'm very sorry you had to drive all the way down here from the City," she said handing him a business card. "My private number is on the back. In the future, you can just call me with your report."

Pierce took the card and put it in his jacket pocket.

"I thought you told me on the phone that Mr. Williams only likes his reports in person."

"Normally that would be the case. However in this instance, Mr. Williams feels it would be more discreet if you called. If he needs to see you, I'll let you know."

"I see."

"I think you should know that Mr. Williams has been ill for some time, so I have been taking care of his day-to-day business affairs."

"So you are aware of my business with your boss?" Pierce asked.

"Yes, I'm well aware, and I must tell you I think you are wasting your time. I have seen nothing amiss. Not with the merchandise or anything else for that matter."

"You would advise me to quit the case?"

"I'm not suggesting that at all. Mr. Williams is worried that there is something going on. If you find nothing, it will help put his mind at ease. Don't worry. He can afford to pay you well for as long as you take to investigate thoroughly."

"Speaking of pay..."

"As you must have surmised, Mr. Williams doesn't care for unnecessary paper work. Would cash be acceptable?"

"Quite acceptable."

"You will find your fee waiting for you at your office before the day is over."

"That won't be necessary. I usually get paid at the end of the week. Fridays usually, but I could use something for expenses in the meantime."

"Would a hundred dollars suffice?"

"That would be fine."

"It will be in your office by the time you return."

"Leave it with the bartender in O'Callaghan's just below my office."

"Very well," Susan Li said. "Please let me escort you to your car."

Once outside, Pierce pointed to the red Mustang.

"Nice looking machine. Looks new."

"Brand new."

"Yours?"

"It belongs to Stacy."

"Stacy?"

"I would think you would have checked out your clients thoroughly. Stacy is Mr. Williams's daughter."

Pierce got in his car and started it. The throaty rumble of the Healey's exhausts came to life.

"Does Stacy live here?" he asked.

"Sometimes."
"What's she like?"
"You're not her type, Mr. Pierce."
"How's that?"
"You're a man," Susan Li said.

CHAPTER FOUR

Paul Chow had been dead for three days when the maid found him. She had gone to his Hong Kong penthouse on Monday morning and let herself in as was her usual routine. She did not think it was strange that the apartment was empty. Dr. Chow often spent his weekends on his yacht in the harbor where he liked to entertain guests. Not until she went to the master bedroom, found the unmade bed, and a bedside lamp knocked over on the floor did she think anything was wrong. She called out to Dr. Chow but heard no reply.

She then carefully opened the door to the master bath and saw Paul Chow in the large tub filled with water and covered with blood. He was still in his pajamas. His face was bloated and had turned blue—the lamp's electrical cord wrapped around his neck.

Susan Li picked up the phone, "Hello."

She listened to a man's voice on the other end of the line. She swallowed hard. The blood drained from her face.

"Are you sure?"

She nodded her head slightly as she listened intently. After a few minutes, she said, "Yes, I understand," and hung up the phone.

She sat behind her executive desk, turned her chair around toward the floor-to-ceiling windows, and looked out at San Francisco's skyline and the Bay beyond from the thirty-fourth floor of her Montgomery Street office. She thought for several minutes before turning back to her desk and pushing the button on the intercom.

"Marcia, call Mr. Frank Pierce. His number is in the Rolodex."

After a few minutes the voice of Susan Li's secretary could be heard on the intercom.

"I'm sorry, Ms. Li, but there's no answer."

"Could you find the number for O'Callahan's, it's a bar on Twenty-fourth Street, and call it."

After two minutes, "There's a gentleman named Mickey O'Callaghan on the line for you, Ms. Li," the intercom voice said.

"Thank you, Marcia."

Susan Li picked up the phone.

"Mr. O'Callahan, this is Susan Li. Mr. Pierce told me he could be reached at this number. Is he there?"

At the other end of the phone, Susan Li could hear the bartender yell, "Pierce, it's for you," and the sound of the handset being placed down on the bar.

She heard Pierce's voice in the background saying, "Set me up again, will ya," then, on the phone, "Frank Pierce."

"Mr. Pierce, this is Susan Li. I have to meet with you as soon as possible."

"Sure, how about in my office," Pierce asked.

"No, I think I would prefer neutral ground."

"Neutral ground? Are we at war?"

The Kiss of the Dragon Lady

"I only just meant somewhere neither of us was well known."

"How about the Tosca Cafe on Columbus in North Beach?"

"No..., let's meet at the bar at the Shadows on Telegraph Hill. Do you know it?"

"I've heard of it."

"It has a wonderful copper bar that overlooks Yerba Buena and Treasure Island. They make a great Gibson. Let's say about eight o'clock."

"That's cutting it a little thin, don't you think. I've got to be at the warehouse tonight, remember?"

"That's one of the things I want to talk to you about. There is no need to continue the surveillance, at least not tonight."

Pierce thought for a moment. What's she up to?

"Okay, you can bring the hundred you owe me. And pay for the drinks."

"The restaurant is on Montgomery across from the Filbert stairs."

"I'm sure I can find it," Pierce said and hung up.

Pierce returned to the far end of the bar to where a shot of Jameson was waiting for him.

"So, now you want me to be your secretary, too," O'Callaghan said.

"I don't know. How's your shorthand?"

"I'll tell you what, Pierce. You pay up your bar bill and I'll tell the next dame that calls for you that you left town."

"It's not like that. That was all business. And you'll be happy to know that I can make good on what I owe you after tonight."

"Un-huh, I'll believe it when I see some green on the

bar," O'Callaghan said.

But Pierce wasn't listening. He was thinking about the meeting with Susan Li. Her voice was different on the telephone. Earlier that afternoon, she was all business, but now there was a softness in her tone that, frankly, sent the hair on the back of his neck on end. Something was wrong. Well, he'd find out what, tonight.

CHAPTER FIVE

At quarter to eight, Pierce walked into the Shadows restaurant and climbed the stairs to the bar. He wanted to arrive early before the meeting, so he could get the lay of the land. He wasn't anticipating anything unexpected, but on the other hand, he didn't like surprises.

He found Susan Li already sitting at the far end of the bar waiting for him. She was still in her dark business suit, but she had added a bright red scarf to her ensemble. And although it was after sunset, she was still wearing sunglasses. He walked over and took the empty stool next to her.

"Good evening, Ms. Li."

"Hello, Frank. It is Frank, isn't it? Let's not be so formal. Please call me Susan."

"All right, if you insist, Susan."

"Let's have a drink, shall we," she said as she signaled the bartender.

The bartender came over.

"Good evening, Mr. Pierce. It's been a long time. I don't think you've been in since...," the bartender said.

"Hello, Sam. It's been a while. I think you know Ms.

Li," Pierce said indicating Susan Li with a nod of his head. "I believe she's a fan of your dry Gibsons if I'm not mistaken."

"It's nice to see you again, Ms. Li. The usual?" Sam asked.

"That'll be fine, Sam," she said.

"And how about you, Mr. Pierce? Jameson on the rocks?" the bartender asked.

Pierce laughed.

"Good memory."

Then, turning his attention to Susan Li, "Neutral ground, I think you said."

"What could be more neutral than a place where we both know the bartender," she said with a warm smile.

"Do you come here often?"

"My wife and I used to come here quite a bit."

"Ah, yes, your wife. You're no longer together, I understand."

"You do your homework, Ms. Li."

"That's my job. And it's Susan, remember?"

"One Beefeater Gibson, extra dry, and a Jameson," Sam said as he set the drinks on the bar.

"What shall we drink to?" Pierce asked as he raised his glass.

Susan Li thought for a moment.

"Let's drink to new beginnings."

"To new beginnings," he said and then they clinked glasses for good luck before touching them to their lips.

"I'm curious. What's with the sunglasses?" Pierce asked.

"I was born with a rare genetic disorder. I'm hyper-photosensitive. I can't stand bright light."

"That must be difficult to live with."

The Kiss of the Dragon Lady

"I've gotten used to it. I've learned to love doing things that one does in the dark," she said.

She paused and took a sip from her Gibson.

"I'm hungry," she said, "and they have the best German food in the City here. What do you say we get a table downstairs? We can talk over dinner, on me of course."

"If you brought my fee, I'll spring for supper," he said.

"How chivalrous of you, Frank. But I'm the client, remember? I'll write it off as a business expense."

"I thought you were avoiding a paper trail?"

"You needn't to worry about that," she said and turned to the bartender. "Sam, could you call downstairs and get us a table for two?"

"That hit the spot," Pierce said as he put his wine glass down on the table after finishing the last of a bottle of Gewürztraminer. "I haven't had good bratwurst and sauerkraut in quite a spell.

"But, we haven't got to why you thought it was so urgent that we meet," Pierce said.

Susan Li finished her wine.

"I know a great place for an after dinner drink not far from here. We can talk there. That is, if you're game."

"That sounds like a challenge."

"I suppose it does, but I didn't mean it that way. I have a proposition for you. One I think you'll like."

Pierce was intrigued even though something deep inside set off an alarm bell warning him to be careful, very careful.

Susan Li was captivating. In fact, she was the most captivating woman he had ever met. Men's eyes followed her and women's eyes were full of envy as she walked ahead of him through the restaurant. Once outside, she led him across the street and down the Filbert Steps to Napier Lane.

"I'm pretty sure there's no place to get a drink down this way," Pierce said.

"Don't be too sure, Frank. We're going to my place."

Pierce's pulse quickened.

They walked down the wooden boardwalk and entered a small, white cottage. Once inside, Pierce could make out the modern decor of leather, chrome, and glass in the dim light. On the far side of the small living room were large windows and French doors that opened out onto a small deck looking out over the Bay. The view of Treasure Island and Yerba Buena Island was much the same as the one from the Shadows's bar.

"Please sit down. I'll get us that drink. I'm going to have a cognac. I'm afraid I don't have any Irish Whiskey. Can I get you something else?"

"How about scotch?"

"I've got a bottle of Ballantine's, I think. Will that work?"

"That'll work fine," Pierce said and sat on the black leather couch.

Susan Li entered the walk-in kitchen and poured the drinks, returned, and set them down on the glass top of the coffee table.

"I'll be back in a moment. I've been in these clothes all day," she said and left the room by ascending a narrow cast-iron, circular stairway that led to what Pierce assumed was the bedroom. He fantasized that she would return down the stairs in a long, black silk negligee.

He was disappointed. When she did return, she was wearing a man's blue oxford dress shirt buttoned to her neck and tucked into a pair of jeans. But there was something else about the way she looked. She had taken off her sunglasses.

She threw a thick manila envelope on the table.

"Here's three thousand dollars. That should settle your account."

"That's a lot of money," he said looking at the envelope. "Your boss only promised me an extra grand when I finished the job."

Susan Li sat beside him on the couch. A dim light from the moonlit sky bathed her face. He looked into her eyes for the first time. They were green. Not black, not brown, but a bright green even in the subdued light. He could not look away. She again gave a slight smile that turned her face into that of a siren.

Pierce couldn't resist her any longer. He took her by the shoulders and pulled her to him. She slipped her arms around his neck, closed her eyes, and parted her lips as he kissed her.

They held their embrace as they kissed each other about the face and neck. He unbuttoned her shirt, found no bra, and kissed her breasts. She let out a muted gasp as he unbuttoned her jeans then helped him slip them from her legs. He kissed her belly, put his hands around her buttocks and buried his head between her legs.

"Not here," she said and struggled to her feet.

He stood and they held each other in their arms. He kissed her. She took his hand and led him up the circular stairs leading to above.

CHAPTER SIX

Pierce woke to find himself covered with just a Paisley print sheet in a king-sized bed. He was alone. They had made love all night, finally falling to sleep in each other's arms after four o'clock.

Paisley just doesn't fit, he thought. Far too cute, too innocent. She's not that kind a woman.

The alarm clock on the bedside table read a few minutes after ten. He stumbled to the bathroom, found his clothes on the floor next to the bed, and dressed.

Downstairs, the envelope was still on the coffee table with a note:

Our mutual acquaintance found your services acceptable; however, they are no longer required. Your compensation in the envelope should take care of everything. Perhaps we shall meet again in the future.

Yours, SL

PS. I hope you had a wonderful time last night. I did.

Pierce picked up the envelope and quickly thumbed

The Kiss of the Dragon Lady

through the cash inside, three thousand in one-hundred dollar bills.

O'Callaghan will be happy, he thought.

He folded Susan Li's note, and shoved it and the envelope into his jacket's inside breast pocket, quickly looked around to see if he had forgotten anything, and left.

The night before, he had parked his car a few blocks away at a metered space on Washington Square and walked up Union Street to the restaurant. As a general rule, he never left the Healey on the street, but last night was definitely a rewarding exception. When he got to his car, he found it undisturbed but with a parking ticket under a wiper blade.

Yes, he thought, absolutely worth it.

Pierce was hungry and decided to grab a corned beef on rye at Harrington's on Larkin Street to take home, so it was almost noon before he got back to his apartment on Noe Street. He took a shower, shaved, and put on fresh clothes before grabbing the corned beef sandwich and heading to O'Callaghan's to wash it down with a Guinness.

"And once again the private dick shows up like a bad penny," O'Callaghan greeted him as he entered the bar.

Pierce didn't say a word. Instead he tossed two one hundred dollar bills on the bar.

"Two C-notes? Who'd you mug, Pierce?"

"An old lady, but she put up a fight. I had to knock her out of her wheelchair. Give me a draft to rinse this down," he said as he unwrapped the corned beef on rye.

O'Callaghan pulled the tap, filling a cold glass, and set the Guinness down in front of Pierce.

H.L. Slater

"You're feeling pretty chipper this afternoon. You must have finally got laid," O'Callaghan said.

Pierce ignored him and took a bite of his sandwich. Then O'Callaghan became serious.

"There was a guy in here asking for you this morning."

"What'd he look like?"

"A guy. What do I know? But he smelled like a cop."

"Probably wanted me to buy tickets to the Policemen's Ball."

But Pierce was worried. With luck, he'd managed to get clear of the jam he'd found himself in, but that didn't mean they couldn't come back at him. Most of the boys hadn't been happy when he testified to the Grand Jury to save his own skin.

"That guy you were asking about the other day, that guy, Williams..."

"Yeah, what about him?"

"Looks like he bumped himself off," O'Callaghan said.

"What? Where'd you hear that?"

"It's in the morning paper."

O'Callaghan picked up the Chronicle off of the backbar and tossed it to Pierce.

"Page four."

Pierce opened the paper. There was a picture of a much younger Williams in an Army Air Corps uniform.

Marcus Williams, noted community leader and World War II veteran, found dead at his Los Altos Hills estate. His body was discovered by his daughter, Stacy Williams, early this morning. A family servant reported that Mr. Williams had been ill for some time, and a small caliber pistol was found near the body in what appears to be a suicide. The police reported that the death is still under investigation.

"Give me a shot of Jameson," Pierce said.

O'Callaghan poured the whiskey and set it on the bar. Pierce downed it.

"What you gave me just about covers your tab. Want me to run you a new one?"

Pierce reached into his wallet and took out another hundred dollar bill and tossed it on the bar.

"Here, put this on my account."

O'Callaghan picked up the three bills and put them in the cash register.

"Now, I know you must've killed somebody."

Pierce was taking a nap on his office couch when he was woken up by a loud knocking. He struggled to his feet and opened the door. He stood face-to-face with Police Sergeant Kevin Flaherty and his partner Inspector John Delaney.

"Well, if it isn't Tweedle Dum and Tweedle Dee. What brings you out in the daylight? Last I heard you guys were running in whores in the Tenderloin."

"Still a smart ass, eh, Pierce. We're working homicide now," Flaherty said.

"What do you two want? You interrupted my beauty sleep."

The two police officers brushed by Pierce and stepped into the office.

"Charming. Please come in. Make yourself at home," Pierce said.

"Sit down. We gotta few questions," Delaney said.

Pierce sat behind his desk and leaned back. He clasped his hands behind his head and propped his feet up on the desk.

"You guys wouldn't happen to have a warrant, would you?"

"Would it make any difference if we did?"

"No, I guess not. Just a friendly chat between old pals. Is that it?"

"Something like that."

"Take your best shot, Flaherty."

"Where were you last night between midnight and five this morning?"

Pierce bolted upright in his chair and put his hands flat on the desk.

"This isn't about the Williams's murder, by any chance?"

"What do you know about it?" Flaherty asked.

"I read it in the morning paper."

"And who said anything about murder?" Delaney added.

"You said you were working homicide. I didn't think you came out here to issue me a parking ticket. That was cute about mentioning suicide to put the killer off guard."

"So answer the question. Where were you?"

"Not that it's any of your business, but I was in the arms of amore."

"You got a name?"

"A gentleman never tells."

"That leaves you out. Better come up with a name or you'll find yourself in deep shit, Pierce," Delaney said.

"You guys know I was working for him, or else you wouldn't be here. But I don't know anything about him other than he was some kind of big shot war hero."

"What were you doing for Williams?" Flaherty asked.

"Just a small job. He thought maybe someone in his

warehouse was moving stuff out the back door. I staked the place out one night but came up empty."

"Just one night?"

"Yeah, just one night. Then he let me go. I figured the problem resolved itself."

"Did you see anything, anyone at the warehouse?"

The Mustang flashed to Pierce's mind.

"Nothing all night. The dock foreman rousted me in the morning, and I left. That was it."

"Caught napping. You're some private dick, Pierce," said Delaney.

"You got nothing on me. If you want to check out my story, talk to Williams's personal secretary, that Susan Li."

"We already tried, but it seems she didn't show up at work this morning. She wasn't with you last night, was she?"

"There's an old saying: 'Keep your dick out of the cash register.' By the way, the paper said Williams bought it down the peninsula. What are you guys doing with it?"

"Marcus Williams was an important public figure here in the City. We're just trying to help out," Flaherty said.

"Yeah, just trying to help out. You guys are just a couple of boy scouts. Now get out of here and let me get back to my nap," Pierce said, got up from his desk, and lay down on the couch again.

After Flaherty and his partner left, Pierce waited a few minutes to be sure the two men didn't return. Then, he jumped up, took Susan Li's card out of his pocket, and dialed her office.

"Good morning, Williams and Chow, Import-Export," said a woman's voice at the other end of the line.

"Good morning, this is Frank Pierce. May I speak to Ms. Li?"

"I'm sorry Mr. Pierce, but Ms. Li won't be in the office today. She's been called away on urgent family business and will be away for some time."

"Do you know where she went? It's very important that I speak with her."

"I'm sorry, sir, but I'm afraid I'm not at liberty to say. I'll tell her you called if I hear from her. Good day," the woman said and hung up.

Pierce flipped Susan Li's business card over and dialed the number on the back. After letting it ring several times, he hung up the phone.

CHAPTER SEVEN

Pierce was debating with himself whether or not to try to get hold of Susan Li at the Williams estate when the phone rang.

"Hello, Susan?" he said.

There was a pause on the other end of the line.

"No. Is this Mr. Pierce, Mr. Frank Pierce?" a girl's voice asked.

"Speaking," Pierce said.

"This is Stacy Williams. My father told me to call you before..., before, he was murdered."

"I was sorry to hear about your father. I didn't know him very well, but he seemed to be a real gentleman."

"You're right. You didn't know him very well. My father was an asshole," Stacy Williams said.

Pierce didn't say anything for a moment, waiting for her to continue.

"And you say, your father told you to call me? What about?" Pierce asked.

"We can't talk over the phone. I'll have to meet you."

Pierce was hesitant. The simple surveillance assignment had turned into a murder case, and he was a prime suspect. The visit from Flaherty and Delaney had more or less said so. The cops would leave it at his door, if they had a chance.

"I don't think that's a good idea, Ms. Williams."

"But my father said I should call you if anything happened to him."

"I don't know why your father would say such a thing. I only met him twice, and then he paid me off."

"Please, I have nobody else to turn to."

After much pleading and against his better judgement, Pierce finally agreed to meet with Stacy Williams.

"How about in Golden Gate Park in front of Kezar Pavilion?" Stacy asked.

"When?"

"Can you make it in an hour?"

Pierce checked his watch. It was twenty minutes to two.

"Let's make it an hour and a half," he said.

Again, he wanted to check out the scene before the meeting. He'd slip a tail if there was one, which he doubted, and see if anyone was following her.

"How will I recognize you?" he asked.

"I'll wear flowers in my hair," she said and hung up.

Pierce walked downstairs and into O'Callahan's and called for a taxi to pick him up on Castro at Twenty-second Street. He left the bar by the rear door, which opened into a common rear yard, and left by the tradesmen's alley of the apartment building on the corner of Castro and Twenty-fourth Streets. He walked up the steep Castro Street hill, wishing he had told the dispatcher Twenty-third. He was still out of breath when the Yellow Cab came over the top of the hill. He hailed the taxi and told the driver to go around the block and drive out Haight

The Kiss of the Dragon Lady

Street to Golden Gate Park.

Haight Street was filled with people, mostly young men and women, dressed in colorful flower print or tie-dye shirts, blue jeans, and buckskin vests covered with fringe, the unofficial uniform of the counter-culture.

"Look at all these hippies," the cab driver said. "Just kids. They come from all over the country just to drop acid and get high at a love-in in the park."

"Maybe I was born too soon," Pierce said.

"It all looks like fun now, but you wait. The pushers and the junkies will move in and devour these flower children and everything will turn to crap, you'll see."

"Yeah, you're probably right. They better enjoy it while it lasts. Drop me at Stanyan."

Pierce paid the driver and walked across Stanyan Street to the park. He checked as nonchalantly as possible to see if he had been followed. He didn't see anyone. Young men and women were sitting around on the grass in groups. Some were playing guitars or recorders. Back farther from the street, a few couples were making out. Just about everyone was smoking marijuana in hand-rolled paper. One could get high just standing around. He felt out of place in his corduroy jacket, khakis, and button-down shirt. He was sure everyone thought he was a cop of some sort. And why shouldn't they, he had been a cop, hadn't he?

He walked up Stanyan to the Kezar Pavilion. Flowers in her hair? She could be any one of the many young women on the street.

"You must be Frank Pierce," a girl's voice came from behind.

Pierce turned around to face a girl dressed in tie-dye and buckskin. She wore a beaded headband and appeared to be no more that eighteen.

"Am I that obvious?"

"Uh-huh. You look like a narc."

Stacy stood five feet, four inches tall, slim with straight blond hair to the middle of her back, and bright blue eyes. She had a fresh, wholesome look about her, the kind of girl they put on billboards to sell laundry soap.

"I need your help," she said.

"Let's walk," he said, knowing that it would make it easier to spot anyone following her.

They crossed Kezar Drive and walked to the Carousel in the park where parents and nannies kept careful eyes on their children in the playground. They sat on one of the benches.

"You got a cigarette?" she asked.

"I don't smoke."

"Neither do I," she said and paused before continuing.

"Su-Li murdered my father," Stacy said.

Pierce considered this revelation for a moment.

"What makes you think that?"

"I know it, that's all. And she's disappeared. That should tell you something."

"That proves nothing. Maybe she had a family emergency or something."

"The only family she has is in China. Besides I heard her arguing with my father."

"What about?"

"I'm not sure exactly, but whatever it was, it was important. Something about a missing shipment. My father kept yelling at Su-Li telling her that she had better do something about it and damn quick, or else there would be hell to pay."

"Do you remember anything else?"

The Kiss of the Dragon Lady

"Your name was mentioned."

"My name?"

"My father wanted to hire a private investigator to find out if the missing shipment ever made it to the warehouse. But she was dead set against it. She didn't want anyone else to get involved who couldn't be trusted."

"You said my name was mentioned."

"My father said he knew of someone, an ex-cop, who could be trusted. He said you had gotten into trouble when you worked in Chinatown and rather than rat out your partner, you kept your mouth shut and lost your job."

"But the first time I ever met your father was the day before yesterday."

"He was a Police Commissioner. Maybe he met you then."

"If so, I don't remember him. I never dealt with the Commission. At least, not directly. Are you sure he was talking about me?"

"When Su-Li insisted in knowing who he wanted to hire, he told her a street smart cop named Frank Pierce, who was wise to the underbelly of Chinatown. Then she asked how he could be so sure you'd keep quiet if the shit hit the fan. He said that if you didn't keep your mouth shut, you'd end up in prison where you wouldn't win the most popular inmate award."

Pierce got to his feet.

"Let's walk," he said.

They continued on the path that led them back to Stanyan Street without so much as a word.

Until Pierce asked, "What do you want from me, Ms. Williams?"

"Isn't it obvious? Find out who killed my father."

"I would imagine that you stand to inherit a great deal

money. Isn't that true?"

"Yeah, I guess so. But what does that got to do with anything?"

"The police will look at who has anything to gain by your father's death. That makes you a suspect."

"They wouldn't think that I'd kill my own father, would they?"

"Patricide is not unheard of, especially when money is involved. Were you at home when your father was murdered?"

"No, I wasn't," she said.

"Then would you mind telling me where you were?"

"At a friend's."

"And might I ask, who is this friend?"

"She's just a friend. She had nothing to do with it."

"She has everything to do with it. You may need her as an alibi for one thing. Were you with her all night?"

"Yes."

"Where does she live?"

"Why?"

"I just told you why. I need to talk to her."

Stacy thought about it.

"I'll talk to her. There's no reason to get her involved unless I have to. I told you Su-Li is who the police should be looking for."

"Maybe so, but the cops aren't going to waste time chasing after her until they're sure you're in the clear."

"Yeah, let me worry about that. I just want you to find Su-Li."

"Your father paid me two hundred a day plus expenses. Does that work for you?"

"I can handle it," Stacy said and handed a slip of paper to Pierce with her phone number on it.

40

The Kiss of the Dragon Lady

"You realize you can't touch your father's money until everything is settled."

"You don't have to worry about getting your money. I've got a trust fund that's all mine. You said my father paid you. When?" she asked.

"When he fired me."

Pierce knew better than to tell Stacy anything about being with Susan Li the night of the murder. Things were bad enough without sending a signal that maybe he and Susan Li were involved. He knew one thing for sure. He had to find Susan Li.

The afternoon was getting late. Pierce checked his watch. It was already past three o'clock. Leaving Stacy on Stanyan where she found him, he hailed a taxi and got in.

"Where to?" the driver asked.

Pierce retrieved Susan Li's card from his wallet.

"Montgomery and Sutter," he said.

The elevator door opened directly into the front office of Williams & Chow, Import-Export, Ltd. Behind the reception desk sat an Asian girl who was surprised to see anyone stepping from the elevator.

"May I help you?" the receptionist asked.

"Good afternoon, I'd like to see Ms. Li," Pierce said.

"I'm sorry, but Ms. Li is away from the office. Did you have an appointment?"

"I'm making an inquiry about the death of Mr. Williams. Is there anyone here that I can talk with?"

"If you're from the police, two officers were already here this morning."

"Yes, Officers Flaherty and Delaney. I'm just doing a follow-up on a small matter that has come up in the investigation."

"Ms. Chow spoke to the officers this morning. I'll see if she is available."

The receptionist picked up the handset on the multi-line call director and pushed the intercom button.

"Ms. Chow, there is another policeman here to see you," she said and returned the handset to its cradle.

Pierce heard a mechanical click of a door lock open.

"You can go in," she said as she got up from behind the desk and opened the door to an inner office.

Once inside, Pierce found another Asian woman behind her desk. An engraved nameplate on her desk read: Marcia Chow, Executive Assistant.

Marcia Chow stood up and extended her hand across her desk to Pierce.

"Good afternoon, Officer...?" she said.

Pierce took the offered hand.

"I'm afraid there has been some misunderstanding. I'm not a police officer. My name is Frank Pierce. I'm a friend of Ms. Li."

"Oh, I see," Marcia Chow said and sat down. "I'm afraid I can't help you, Mr. Pierce. You see, Ms. Li has been called away on an urgent family matter."

"Yes, I know. I was hired by Mr. Williams before his death to investigate some..., some irregularities, and I was hoping to talk with Ms. Li."

"Irregularities?"

"But that's not important. What is important is that Ms. Li and I are friends, and she has been accused of Mr. Williams's murder. I know she is innocent, but I must see her right away."

"Mr. Pierce, you may be trying to help Ms. Li, but I can't help you. The simple fact is that I don't know where she is. She left me a rather cryptic message on my answering machine at home saying she had to get away and not to worry, and that everything would be all right. I didn't know what she meant by that until the two police officers came here this morning."

"If you hear from her, tell her I'm only here to help, but it is urgent that I see her right away."

"I certainly will, Mr. Pierce," she said and came from behind her desk to escort him from the office.

At the door, Pierce turned to her and said, "Your name is Chow? Are you any relation to Paul Chow, Mr. Williams's business partner?"

Marcia Chow smiled.

"Chow is a very common name in China. Goodbye, Mr. Pierce," she said and closed the door behind him.

The receptionist was not at her station. The outer office was empty. He saw a phone line light up on the call director. He picked up the handset and heard Marcia Chow saying, "...urgent that he sees you," before the line went dead.

Pierce reached under the receptionist's desk and found the button that unlocked the door to Marcia Chow's office. She was still hanging on the phone.

"Where is she?" he shouted.

"I don't know. All I have is a number she gave me to call if anyone came looking for her. It's an answering service. I leave a message, and then she calls back."

"What's the number?"

"Here, I'll write it down for you."

Marcia Chow ripped a sheet from the notepad on her desk, wrote down a number, and gave it to him.

"Say you have a message for Mrs. Phillips," she said.

He shoved the number in his pocket and turned to leave.

"Mr. Pierce."

"Yes?" he asked, looking back to Marcia Chow.

"Never mind," she said.

When Pierce left the building, a gray, unmarked Chevy Malibu was parked at the curb. John Delaney was standing beside it.

"Get in, Pierce. I'll give you a lift."

"Where to, down to the Hall?"

"Nah, to wherever you're headed. That okay?"

"Yeah, sure."

Pierce figures Delaney wants to talk, and he should listen to what the Inspector has to say.

Pierce opened the car door and got in as Delaney walked around to the driver's side and slid behind the wheel.

"Where to?" Delaney asked.

"It's been a long day. I was planning to go home and get a good night's sleep."

"Yeah, I'll bet you were," Delaney said as he pulled away from the curb.

"My guess is that this is more than a social call," Pierce said.

"You could say that. What's your business with Susan Li?"

"Not much. She wasn't in."

"That we know. What we want to know is how tight you are with her."

"Strictly business. Williams owed me money for that job I told you about. I was hoping to collect from Li."

Delaney drove up Market Street toward Twin Peaks.

"So, that wasn't you with Li at the Shadows last night," Delaney said.

The Kiss of the Dragon Lady

Fuck, Pierce thought, the police must've been tailing her yesterday. But why? Wasn't Williams still alive when he had met her at the restaurant and later back at her place?

"Yeah, we met for a drink, but she told me she didn't have the money with her. She said to come to the office today."

"So, you decided to take an advance out in trade last night?"

The asshole followed us, Pierce thought. And he was damn good at it, too. I didn't see a thing.

"Would it interest you to know that she left you with just your cock in your hand around three o'clock?" Delaney asked.

Three? Pierce thought. He remembered glancing at the clock on the bedside table. He was sure it read five minutes to four. He was about to tell Delaney about the time, but thought better of it.

"Who called who about the date?" Delaney asked. "You or her?"

"It wasn't a date, and she called me."

"And I bet she also was the one who suggested the restaurant."

"Yeah, so what."

Delaney made a left at Castro Street and drove over the hill toward Twenty-fourth.

"We don't figure you for the murder, but Li has plenty of motive."

"Motive? What motive?"

"Same motive as always in cases like this, money. That's all I can tell you, so don't bother asking."

"I see. You figure she set me up as an alibi, slipped out, and did in her boss."

"She had time, and we got a tip."

Damn it, he thought, Stacy couldn't wait. Spoiled little bitch, she could screw up everything. I need time to figure out what went down.

"A tip, eh? What kind of tip?" Pierce asked.

"You know I can't tell you that."

"Yeah, just leave me off at the corner. I'm going to buy some groceries before I go home."

Delaney pulled the Chevy to the curb at Castro and Twenty-fourth where Pierce got out.

Delaney leaned across the front seat before Pierce closed the door.

"Watch yourself, Pierce. You're in over your head, and you're still not off the hook for the number on Williams. For all we know, you two could've planned this thing together."

"Thanks for the advice," Pierce said and slammed the car door.

Delaney drove away and Pierce walked down the street to O'Callahan's.

CHAPTER EIGHT

When Pierce was growing up, Noe Valley had been almost exclusively made up of working class men and women, mostly of Irish descent, but now the neighborhood was showing signs of gentrification. Workers in white collars were gradually replacing those in blue. Good jobs and a growing economy added to the bright outlook for the future. And although older residents decried the invasion of the pot-smoking hippies, the recent tsunami of children of middle-class American families to the "City of Love" only served to intensify the optimism that spread into neighborhood bars around the city.

Friday night, and O'Callaghan's was packed. Old residents and new arrivals stood elbow to elbow at the bar or at tables against the far wall drinking Irish Whiskey, Bailey's, or Guinness drafted from barrels shipped in from Canada. Pierce squeezed his way to the bar and signaled O'Callaghan.

"Can't you see I'm busy, Frank? What can I get you?"

"Did anyone call for me today?"

"I don't think so..., no, nobody called. What can I get

you to drink?"

"Maybe later. I'll be back."

Pierce made his way back through the crowd to the door. He wanted a drink, but he also wanted peace and quiet. He needed to think. Once he entered his apartment, he went to the kitchen and poured a double shot of Jameson before kicking off his shoes and lying down on the couch. He took a good stiff drink of the whiskey, put the glass on the coffee table, leaned back, and fell asleep.

He dreamed of Rene in her black bikini, except she wasn't Rene any more. She was Susan Li sitting alone on a deserted beach wrapped in a black robe.

He woke up to the urgent buzzing of the downstairs doorbell. It was after dark. He turned on a lamp, stumbled to the door and pushed the intercom button.

"Who is it?"

"It's me," a woman's voice said.

"Who?"

"You know who, please let me in."

He buzzed her in, opened the apartment door, and saw Susan Li coming to the top of the stairs from the lobby. She was dressed in the same dark blue suit as before. She wore a soft cap under which her long, black hair was hidden. Even though it was after dark, she still had on her sunglasses. But even without the hat and sunglasses, Pierce would have recognized her instantly by the way she moved without making a sound, like a jungle cat on the prowl.

"Hurry," Pierce said holding the apartment door open.

She entered and he closed the door behind her.

"Where have you been? Do you know the police are looking for you? They think you killed Williams."

"I know," she said. "Do you think I could have a

drink?"

"All I have is whiskey," he said.

"That'll work."

He went to the kitchen and grabbed the bottle of Jameson and another glass.

"Do you want ice?" he asked from the kitchen.

"Straight will be fine."

Pierce returned to the living room and handed the whiskey to Susan Li. She took a healthy swallow before sitting down on the couch.

"Thank you, I needed that," she said.

"Where have you been? The police want to question you."

"Yes, I'm sure they do. Frank, I didn't kill Williams," she said.

"I know you didn't, darling," he said.

Darling. It had just slipped out. At first, he hadn't realized he had said it, but in that moment, his feelings about Susan Li crystallized. He sat down close to her.

"How did you know where I live?"

"You've got to be kidding. I know everything about you Francis Xavier Pierce."

"Nobody's called me Francis Xavier since the nuns at St. Paul's."

"I never met an Irishman named Frank that wasn't a Francis Xavier."

"No, I guess not."

Susan Li took another drink of of her whiskey.

Pierce let her relax a bit longer before he asked again, "Where have you been?"

"I went into hiding as soon as I heard that Williams was found dead. I knew that the police would want to ask me questions. Questions I didn't want to answer."

"So, where did you go?"

"I've been staying with a friend in Chinatown."

Chinatown, why is it always Chinatown? Pierce asked himself.

"Well, you can't stay here. The cops think I might've helped you murder Williams, and I don't know what else. You took a big risk coming here. That wasn't smart."

"I was careful. I waited down the street until I was sure you weren't being watched. Besides, the police aren't the ones that I'm worried about, and there were men asking around Chinatown if anyone had seen me. I had to get out of there."

"Well, staying here is out, but I might have a solution."

Pierce checked his watch.

"It's only ten o'clock. We'll have to lie low here for a few hours before I can find out."

"Whatever you say. I've been in these clothes three days now. Mind if I take a shower?"

"The bathroom is the first door on the right as you came in. There are fresh towels in the hall closet next to the door."

"Thank you," she said as she stood up, straightening the creases in her skirt.

Pierce watched her as she walked across the room and down the short hall, her hips gently swaying with each step.

God, she's beautiful, he thought.

He sat with his drink listening to the water running in the shower. Then it stopped. After several minutes, the bathroom door opened, and Susan Li came to the living room wrapped in a white towel with another around her hair. Her green eyes bored into his.

"I'm going to lie down," she said, letting the towel fall

The Kiss of the Dragon Lady

to the floor before she turned, and walked back into the bedroom opposite the bath.

In the bedroom, Susan Li was already under a white sheet with her head on a pillow. In the faint light filtering in from the street, she watched as he undressed, tossing his clothes across a plain wooden chair.

He went to the nightstand, opened the drawer, and took out a Smith & Wesson Stub-nose .38 and put it on the bedside table before slipping under the sheet and pulling Susan Li to him.

"Just hold me and don't let go," she said.

They held each other as if fused as one.

"Promise me," she said. "Never let go."

They fell asleep in each other's arms. When Pierce woke, it was nearly two a.m. He got up quietly, trying not to disturb Susan Li, but she woke from her restless sleep as he was dressing.

"Where are you going?" she asked.

"I have to go find out about where you can hide until we get everything straightened out. We can't risk using the telephone. We don't know who could be listening."

"How long will it take?"

"Not long. Don't turn on any lights. And if anyone should come to the door, don't answer it no matter who they say they are. I'm leaving my gun here on the table. Do you know how to use it?"

"Cock, point, and pull the trigger."

After he was dressed, he leaned across the bed and kissed her.

"Don't worry. Everything will be okay," he said.

She heard the click of the front door lock. She was alone.

* * *

Pierce left by the rear door of the apartment building and slipped out the tradesmen's alley. He checked the front for any signs of life before stepping into the street. He stayed close to the buildings as he walked down Noe Street on his way to O'Callahan's.

By the time he got to the bar, it was after closing time. He knocked on the door. No answer. He knocked again, this time more loudly.

"We're closed. Go home," he heard O'Callaghan yell.

"It's Pierce. Open up. I need to talk to you."

O'Callaghan came to the door and opened it a little way.

"What'd ya want, Pierce?"

"Let me in. I need a favor."

"What kind of favor?"

"Let me in damn it. It's cold out here."

O'Callaghan started to open the door to let Pierce in just as a shot rang out making a bullet hole in the bar's front door. Pierce dove through the doorway dragging O'Callaghan to the floor with him.

"What the fuck!" O'Callaghan said after they heard car tires squeal away.

"Don't worry. They couldn't miss at that range. That was just meant to scare me off," Pierce said.

"I don't know about you, but it did a good job on me. I need a drink," O'Callaghan said.

They got up off the floor, and O'Callaghan went behind the bar and poured two shots of Jameson. They downed the whiskey, and O'Callaghan refilled the glasses.

"How do you know somebody doesn't want you dead?" O'Callaghan asked.

"Dead cops, even ex-cops like me, are bad for business. Makes other cops shoot first and spell out Miranda rights as an afterthought."

"And what business are we talking about here?"

"I don't know, not yet anyway, but I know it must have to do with Williams's murder."

"I warned you not to get involved with that guy."

"Well, it looks like you were right, but right now I need a favor."

"What kind of favor?"

"You know your beach house down in Montara? I need to borrow it for a few days."

"You thinking of laying low until whoever stops shooting at you?"

"It's for..., for a client. She needs to keep out of sight until I can figure out what's going on."

"She, eh? Sounds like you're thinking with your dick again."

"What do you mean by that?"

"Oh, nothing. Forget I said it."

"Well, how about it? Can I use beach house?"

"Sure, I'll get the key in the office."

O'Callaghan went to the back room behind the bar, returned with the key, and handed it to Pierce.

"You know what I said about you not being smart? Well, you haven't done anything to change my mind," O'Callaghan said.

"Thanks, I'll get the key back to you in a couple of days."

"How about the bullet hole in my front door, Pierce?"

"I'd leave it, gives the joint character," Pierce said on his way out.

This time Pierce wasn't cautious. He hurried back to his building, bounded up the stairs, and unlocked the door to his apartment.

"Hurry up and get dressed. We've got to get out of here," he shouted as he entered the dark apartment.

"What's the rush, Pierce?"

He turned on a table lamp and found Sergeant Flaherty sitting on the couch. Pierce checked the bedroom. The bed was empty.

"Looking for your little Chinese girlfriend? She ain't here," Flaherty said.

"I don't know what you're talking about, Flaherty."

"Don't play dumb. We both know she was here."

"Oh, yeah? Where'd you hear that?"

"A little bird told me. I never thought that you were the smartest cop I ever worked with, but hiding a fugitive, you should know better."

"Fugitive?"

"Let's just say she's someone we'd like to talk to. And in case you're worried, this time I've got a warrant."

"How'd you get in?"

"The door was unlocked. You should know better. Someone could come in and rob you."

Flaherty stood up and went to the door.

"I hope she was good," he said. "Where you're going, you'll have a lot of time to remember, or trying to forget."

As soon as Flaherty was gone, Pierce went into the bedroom. His gun wasn't in the nightstand. He looked around the bed and the dresser, but it was nowhere to be found.

Fuck! he thought, now she's got my gun.

There wasn't anything he could do at that hour of the morning, so he went back to bed, hoping Susan Li would return. But she only reappeared in a black bikini sitting on

The Kiss of the Dragon Lady

the beach, alone, when he closed his eyes.

At nine o'clock, he got up, took a shower, shaved and grabbed a cup of coffee in the kitchen. He took his car out of the garage and drove out to Forty-sixth Avenue and Judah in the Sunset. Big Leo, who weighs three hundred and fifty pounds if he weighs and ounce, was behind the counter when Pierce stepped into Markell's Gun Shop.

"Can I help you...? Well, look who the cat dragged in," Big Leo said.

"Hey, Leo, it's been awhile."

"You can say that again. What, I haven't seen you in five, maybe six years. Then you and your old partner stop in within days of each other."

"Yeah? Which one? I've had a few over the years."

"Kevin Flaherty came in last week."

"Now that's a coincidence. Kev and I just saw each other. And we plan to get together again real soon."

"Good to see you guys are still friends after all that went down."

"That's all water under the bridge. Kev and I were partners for a long time. What was he doing here? Just stopping in to say hello?"

"He picked up a small .32 automatic for a friend. Said she lived alone and thought she should have some protection. Can I show you anything? Or were you just in the neighborhood?"

"I don't know if you heard, but I went into the private eye racket. Pretty much low key stuff, petty larceny, divorces, you know, that kind of thing."

"So, I guess you're looking for a piece."

"I don't usually carry nowadays, but some guys can get pretty nasty when they find out their old lady's been riding somebody else's pony. My service revolver's too big. I

55

need something smaller in case one of these guys gets out of hand."

"Sounds reasonable. What've you got in mind?"

"A Smith and Wesson .38 Special stub nose. Small enough to carry under my coat, but with a big enough punch if I ever need it."

"Looking for new or used?"

"New. I want one that hasn't had its cherry popped."

"I've got just what you need right here. Brand new, never been fired," Leo said.

He opened the display case, took out the weapon and handed it to Pierce. Pierce felt the gun's heft in his hand.

"This'll do fine. Wrap it up. And you better give me a box of shells with it."

"How'd you like to pay, Frank?"

"How's cash sound?"

"Sounds just fine to me."

"And Leo could you do me a favor and lose the paperwork for a while before you report it to the Department?"

"Your partner said the same thing. You cops are all the same. Don't want the bosses to know you've got a throw away."

"Well, you never know who you're going to run into. There are some nuts out there that you don't even remember busting that have a hard-on for you."

"Yeah, I guess."

Pierce paid in cash and took a package with the gun and bullets inside.

"Can I ask you for another favor?"

"What is it?"

"I'm going to have dinner with Kev next week. If you see him, don't tell him I was in. I want to see the expression on his face when I tell him that you and I got together like old times."

"Sure, Frank, sure."

Big Leo knew that was bullshit, but he would keep his mouth shut. Nobody in his business wants to get the reputation of being a blabbermouth.

CHAPTER NINE

Pierce pulled over to the curb opposite a payphone on Judah Street and turned off his engine. He unwrapped the .38, loaded it, and stuck it in his belt holster before getting out of the Healey to call Stacy. He slipped a dime into the phone slot, looked at the slip of paper Stacy had given him, and dialed the number.

The phone at the other end rang several times before a girl's husky voice answered.

"Hello?"

"Hello, is Stacy there?" Pierce asked.

"Who wants to know?"

"Tell her it's Frank Pierce."

He could hear the husky voice calling to someone in the background, "Hey, sweetcheeks, there's a guy on the phone for you." Then into the phone again, "Who'd you say you were?"

"Pierce, Frank Pierce. She's expecting a call from me."

He heard the sound of the phone being set down on a table or countertop and then in the background.

"Says his name's Pierce. Get your ass out of bed. I ain't your fuckin' secretary."

The Kiss of the Dragon Lady

After a minute of indistinct chatter in the background, Stacy came on the line.

"Hello, Mr. Pierce?"

"Good morning, Stacy. I hope I didn't wake you," he said.

"We weren't sleeping. What've you got for me?"

He quickly put the image of Stacy standing naked at the other end of the phone out of his mind.

"I've got a line on Susan Li, but it hasn't panned out so far. And the cops are looking for her, too. They came to my joint thinking I knew something."

"Did you tell them about me?"

"Your name never came up. And there's some kind of rule about mentioning a client's name to the cops."

"Why'd you call if you don't have anything?"

"I'm just checking in. Have you thought of anything that can help me find her?"

"Maybe you should ask around Chinatown. I know she spent a lot of time there."

Sure, Pierce thought, that's just where I should be seen snooping around..., if I want my nuts handed to me on a platter.

"Any place special in Chinatown?" he asked.

"There's a restaurant she used to like to go to. Sam Wong's, or something like that. I think it's on Washington Street off of Grant."

"You mean, Sam Wo's?"

"Yeah, that's it. She likes to go there for a late night supper after she's been out on the town," Stacy said.

"I'll check it out. Anything else?"

"I'll call you if I can think of anything. Goodbye," she said and hung up.

Pierce fished in his pocket, found another dime, and

called the number that Marcia Chow had given him for Susan Li's answering service.

"Good morning, answering service. How shall I direct your call?" came a young man's voice over the phone.

"Mrs. Phillips, please," Pierce said.

"I'm sorry, sir. Mrs. Phillips is not in her office just now. Would you like to leave a message?"

"Tell her Pierce called, and I need to talk with her as soon as possible."

"Certainly sir. What is your number, Mr. Pierce?"

"She has it," he said and hung up.

The sun was breaking through as the morning fog receded toward the ocean. Pierce put the top down on the Healey, made a U-turn in the middle of the street and drove across town to Telegraph Hill. He was lucky to find a parking place at the top of Union Street at Montgomery from where it was an easy walk down the Filbert Steps to Napier Lane.

He found the cottage again without difficulty and knocked on the door. There was no answer. He tried the doorknob, but it was locked. He knocked again.

"If you're looking for the lady that lives there, she left this morning."

Pierce turned to see the smiling face of a woman in her seventies standing on the boardwalk in front of the cottage. She wore a wide-brimmed straw hat, and on one arm she carried an empty basket for cut flowers, and in her hand, pruning shears.

"You say she left? Would you happen to know where she was going?" he asked.

"She didn't say, son, but she was carrying a suitcase. Going to be gone a spell, I reckon," the woman said.

The Kiss of the Dragon Lady

Pierce had thought about forcing the door, but that wasn't an option with the woman in the straw hat standing there. He reached into his pocket and took out a business card with his name and office number on it and handed it to the woman.

"If Ms. Li comes back could you give her this card and tell her it's urgent that I speak with her," he said.

"Ms. Li? I don't know any Ms. Li. You must have the wrong address. My friend, Marcia Chow lives here, has for a long time."

"Miss Chow? Marcia Chow?"

"That's right. She's been here for years."

"Thanks, if Miss Chow comes back, please give her my card," he said and hurried off.

He took the Filbert Steps two at a time. When he reached Montgomery Street, he stopped to catch his breath before continuing farther up the hill to where he left his car.

It was Saturday, so he figured the office of Williams & Chow would be closed. But he knew he was playing catch up on whatever was going on, and something told him he better leave no stone unturned.

Parking was easy as the Financial District was always nearly deserted on weekends. To his surprise, the elevator door opened on the thirty-fourth floor. He found the receptionist behind her desk.

She looked up and smiled. "May I help you?"

"Is Ms. Chow in?"

"You're the police officer who was here before, aren't you?"

"You remember me."

"I'm sorry, but Ms. Chow is not in today."

"Mind if I look for myself," he said and stepped toward

the inner office door.

The receptionist attempted to block Pierce's way.

"I'm sorry, sir, but this office is private."

Pierce reached into the breast pocket of his jacket and pulled out Susan Li's folded note and waved it in the receptionist's face.

"I have a warrant," he said as he brushed by her and pushed the hidden button that unlocked the inner-office door.

The receptionist followed him into the office. She watched him as he looked around. Everything seemed in order, nothing out of place. Another door led into an adjoining room.

"Where's that door lead?" he asked.

"That's Ms. Li's private office."

Pierce went to the door and tried the handle, but it was locked.

"Where's the key?"

"I don't know."

"Well, you better make a damn good guess before I have to break the door in."

"Try the middle drawer," she said pointing to the desk.

He looked in the drawer and found the key and let himself into the room. A sweeping view of the City and the Bay framed Susan Li's black leather executive chair and chrome and glass desk. Everything looked proper, nothing out of place. He noticed a fireplace at the far side of the room. Above the mantelpiece was an oil portrait of Marcus Williams, dressed in the uniform of an Army Major. The picture frame was held out slightly from the wall. Upon a closer inspection, Pierce found the picture frame was hinged to swing out. Behind the portrait was a wall safe with its door ajar. He looked inside and found it empty.

He turned to the receptionist who was standing in the doorway with her arms folded tightly in front of her. He took a closer look at her face for the first time. She seemed somehow familiar. Had he seen her somewhere before?

She was dressed in a plain tan dress, buttoned up the front all the way to her chin. She had on only light makeup, and her hair was pulled back and held in place with tortoise shell side combs. He could see she was really quite attractive behind her carefully planned exterior.

"What is your name?" Pierce asked.

"Linda Hsieh."

"Sit down, Ms. Hsieh," he said indicating a black leather chair in front of the desk.

Linda Hsieh sat down, her back straight, her knees together, with her hands clasped in her lap.

She reminded him of the girls in their parochial uniforms sitting at mass in Saint Paul's on Fridays before being discharged into the sinful world for the weekend.

"I'm sure you are aware that Mr. Williams was murdered...,

She nodded her head.

"...and I'm looking into the matter. Both Ms. Li and Ms. Chow are people we want to talk with to help us find the person or persons responsible. They are not suspects, but we feel that they may have information that could further our investigation.

"I was surprised to find the office open today. Are you usually open on Saturdays?"

Linda Hsieh shook her head and said, "No, not usually."

"And how is it that you happen to be here this

Saturday?"

Linda Hsieh squirmed in her chair, reminding him again of the girls in church just before going into the confessional.

Father forgive me, for I have sinned...

"I remind you that murder is very serious crime. You could be in big trouble if you don't tell me everything you know."

"I don't know anything about any murder or anything else. I just answer the telephone and keep track of appointments when people visit the office. That's all."

"And where do you keep track of these appointments?"

"In a book in my desk," she answered.

"I'll have to look at that book," he said.

"You can't. It's not here," she said.

"It's not here. Why isn't it here?"

"Ms. Chow took it with her before you came."

"You mean this morning?"

"She called me early and told me to meet her here. She said she couldn't find her elevator key, and she needed some important files that she'd left in the office."

"So you met her here and opened the office. What did she do then?"

"She went into her office. I guess she got her files. She wasn't in there very long."

"And your appointment book?"

"She took it and put it into a small suitcase she had with her."

"Then what?"

"She called a taxi and left."

"So why didn't you leave?"

"I went to the bathroom. I was about to go, but you came in."

The Kiss of the Dragon Lady

Pierce went back to the elevator and pushed the call button. Linda Hsieh followed him.

"How long ago did she leave before I got here?"

"Only a few minutes," she said.

The elevator door opened. Pierce entered and pushed the button for the Lobby.

As soon as the elevator door closed, Linda Hsieh picked up the phone and dialed.

"That cop Pierce was here. He just left," she said into the phone.

"No, I didn't tell him anything, I swear."

She listened on the phone for a moment.

"I couldn't help it. He barged right in, but he didn't find anything."

She listened again.

"I won't, I promise," Linda Hsieh said and hung up.

Pierce figured that Marcia Chow would head back to her place. He hurried to his car, and headed back to Telegraph Hill. He couldn't find a place to park right away. Finally he found a spot farther down Union Street and walked the rest of the way.

He greeted the lady in the straw hat near the top of the Filbert Steps. She was bent over tending the flowerbeds.

"Good morning again," he said.

The woman looked up.

"Afternoon, I think you mean," she said.

He glanced at his watch.

"Do you know if Ms. Chow returned?"

The woman straightened her back, put her hands on her hips, and stretched.

"Nope, haven't seen her. Might've come back while I was in the house getting some potting soil."

"Thanks, I'll check," Pierce said and continued on down the steps to Napier Lane.

Pierce knocked on the door of the cottage but got no answer. Through the door he heard music,

...*I'd love to turn you on...*

He tried the door and this time found it unlocked. He opened it slowly and put his head inside.

"Ms. Chow?"

There was no response. He raised his voice.

"Ms. Chow?"

Still nothing.

Pierce went to the kitchen where he found Marcia Chow lying on the floor in a pool of blood.

...*somebody spoke and I went into a dream...*

He turned off the radio on the kitchen counter. He didn't bother being careful. He knew his fingerprints were everywhere, left behind after his tryst with Susan Li. Still, he didn't want to pick up the telephone in case someone else's prints were on it.

He quickly looked around the cottage for the small suitcase, even running upstairs to check the closets, but he found nothing. Then he went outside and found the lady in the straw hat.

"I'm sorry to bother you. I don't even know your name, but can I use your telephone?"

"I'm Alice Blount. What's yours?"

"Pierce, Frank Pierce. I'm a private investigator. I used to be with the Police Department."

"You got any I.D.?"

He took out his wallet and showed her his Investigator's license.

"Okay, come with me," she said and led him into another small cottage near Marcia Chow's.

The Kiss of the Dragon Lady

He picked up the phone and dialed the number he knew by heart. The phone rang a few times before someone answered.

"Hello, Kathy. This is Frank Pierce. Can I speak to Kevin?"

There was a moment of silence at the other end of the phone.

"He's not here. He went into work this morning."

"Thanks," he said, but the line had gone dead.

He tapped the hook on the phone to get a dial tone and dialed another number.

"Give me homicide," he said into the phone.

Then after a moment, he heard, "Homicide, McGarrity."

"Let me talk to Flaherty."

"He ain't here, it's Saturday. You want to speak to his partner?"

"Yeah, okay."

"Who's calling?"

"Tell him it's Frank Pierce."

Pierce could hear McGarrity through the phone, "Hey, Delaney, guess who wants to talk to you? That asshole, Pierce. Pick up the phone."

After several moments Delaney picked up the phone.

"What do you want, Pierce?"

"I've got another body for you, Delaney. I'll meet you in Napier Lane, and bring the dusters."

"What's the address?"

"I'm not sure it has one. It's a white cottage. I'll be in front," he said and hung up.

Alice Blount had been listening to his end of the conversation.

"What's wrong? Is Marcia okay?"

Pierce turned to Alice Blount.

"I'm sorry, but I'm afraid she's dead. The police will be here in a few minutes, and they will want to ask you a few questions."

"I liked her, but I'm not surprised if something bad has happened to her."

"Why would you say that?"

"Strange people were always coming and goin', mostly at night."

"What kind of people? Men, women? White, Asian, Black?"

"Men mostly. Never seen no black people, just whites and Chinamen."

"When the police get here, just answer them truthfully, and everything will be all right," Pierce told her.

Pierce and Alice Blount waited outside of Marcia Chow's cottage. Inspector John Delaney didn't take long to arrive, followed by a team from Forensics.

"What've you got, Pierce?" Delaney asked.

"This is Alice Blount, a neighbor. I'm sure you'll have some questions for her."

Delaney nodded to Alice Blount.

"Don't go anywhere, Ms. Blount. I'll talk to you in a minute. Right now I want to see Mr. Pierce alone."

Delaney followed Pierce inside the cottage. While the forensics team went over the crime scene, Pierce told Delaney everything just the way it happened from the time of his first arrival that morning.

"Why were you here in the first place?" Delaney asked.

"I'm trying to find Susan Li. When I talked with Chow, just before you picked me up in front of Williams's office yesterday, I had a feeling she knew more than she was letting on. I figured if I could talk to her away from work, she might loosen up."

"How'd you know where to find her?"

"She gave me her address."

"She gave you her home address? Now why would she do that?"

Pierce knew he had fucked up. He had to think fast.

"Look what we have here," said one of the crime scene investigators holding a Smith & Wesson .38 dangling by its trigger guard from a ballpoint pen. "Looks like we won't have a problem finding the murder weapon."

"You wouldn't happen to have your weapon on you, would you Pierce?"

Pierce opened his jacket to show his holstered revolver.

The crime scene investigators completed their work, and Delaney questioned Alice Blount.

"Seems the victim hasn't been dead very long. We'll have the exact time of death after the boys go over her in the lab. But your story checks out with the witness's. You're free to go, Pierce... at least for now."

"You're a sweetheart, Delaney," Pierce said.

When Pierce got back to his car, he found two parking tickets on the windshield.

Pierce figured that whoever killed Marcia Chow had been waiting in the cottage the first time he had knocked on the door that morning. The only person whom he knew for sure that had intimate knowledge of Marcia Chow's cottage was Susan Li. However, the most damning evidence was that when the Forensics Office held up the suspected murder weapon, Pierce recognized his missing revolver.

He didn't want to believe it, but everything pointed to

Susan Li as Marcia Chow's murderer and probably to the murder of Williams, too. Still, something in the back of his head was telling him that things didn't add up. First, the two killings were done with different weapons. Susan Li didn't have his gun when Williams was killed, and the gun that killed Williams was found at the body. Second, in his experience, a gunshot to the temple was a killer's message, a warning of some kind. But a warning to whom and for what?

Pierce would have to move fast. As soon as it was discovered that Marcia Chow's murder was committed with his gun and that his fingerprints were all over the cottage, he would be arrested.

First thing he had to do was to hide his car. The green Healey was too easily recognized. It was risky, but he had no choice. He drove home and put his car in the garage. Then, he went to O'Callahan's.

Only a few customers were at the bar drinking pints of Guinness draft.

"Mickey, I need the keys to the van again," Pierce said as he walked up to the bar.

"Yeah, and good afternoon to you, too."

"Sorry, Mickey, but I'm in a hurry."

"You look like you could use a drink, Pierce."

"Okay, but make it quick."

O'Callaghan poured a shot of Jameson, set it on the bar, and went to the office for the keys. When he returned, he tossed them on the bar.

"Thanks, Mickey."

"Wait a minute. I almost forgot. I guess I'm your fucking secretary after all. A woman called for you..."

"Did she leave her name?"

"She just said to tell you that Sam is a mutual friend."

The Kiss of the Dragon Lady

"How about a number?"

"Yeah, it's on the register."

O'Callaghan ripped a piece of paper from a notepad next to the cash register and handed it to Pierce.

"Let me use the phone," Pierce said.

O'Callaghan put the phone on the bar. Pierce looked at the piece of paper but didn't recognize the number. He picked up the phone and dialed. He let the phone ring twenty times before he hung up, downed the shot of whiskey, and headed for the door.

"Thanks, Mickey," he said. "I'll get the van back as soon as I can."

Pierce wanted to think, so he took the Coast Highway down to Montara. Along the way he stopped in Linda Mar to fill his gas tank and buy some groceries, including a bottle of Jameson and a bottle of Beefeater Gin. He tried calling the phone number again from a booth outside a small grocery and filling station. After letting it ring, there still was no answer.

He found O'Callaghan's beach house just off the highway up a hundred yards from the beach. There wasn't much to it, two rooms, a walk-in kitchen, and small bathroom with a shower. But the beach house was comfortable and had a fireplace.

By the time he settled in, the summer fog was already drifting in from the Pacific, lowering the temperature several degrees. He put some kindling and three small logs in the fireplace and attempted to start a fire. After much coaxing and a half of a small box of matches, he managed to get a fire started.

He poured a glass of Jameson, drank half of it, and lay down on a couch in front of the fire. He soon fell asleep.

He was awoken by the telephone ringing. Fog had swept in from the sea and engulfed the cabin. The room was dark with but a faint light filtering in between dark curtains. Next to the couch, he found a table lamp with the phone next to it. He turned on the light, picked up the phone, and listened without speaking.

"Pierce?"

Pierce recognized O'Callaghan's voice.

"Yeah, Mickey, I'm here."

"Thought you'd like to know. Two cops were in here looking for you. One was your old partner, Flaherty."

"What did you tell them?"

"Told 'em I hadn't seen hide nor hair of you."

"Anything else?"

"One left a card. Name's Delaney. You know him?"

"Yeah, I know him."

"Told me to tell you to call him if I should happen to run into you. He said you were in a jam, but he could help."

"I'll bet he did."

"Oh, yeah, and that woman called again. Wants to talk to you real bad. She left another number. Got a pen?"

"Just a minute."

Pierce reached into his jacket pocket and found his pen and the paper Stacy Williams had given him.

"Shoot," he said.

He took down the number and looked at it. This one he recognized. It was the same as the other number on the paper, the one belonging to Stacy Williams.

"You sure this is the same woman that called earlier?" he asked.

"She said she had called earlier, so I figured she must be the same one." O'Callaghan said.

The Kiss of the Dragon Lady

"Thanks," Pierce said and hung up.

If it was Stacy who called, how did she know to call O'Callaghan's? If it was Susan Li, what was she doing at Stacy's? He didn't want to take a chance that the number was being traced, so he went to the van and drove back to the phone booth outside the grocery store and dialed Stacy's number.

"Who's this?" the husky voice asked.

"Pierce. Let me speak to Stacy."

He heard indistinct voices as if a hand was placed over the mouthpiece before someone answered.

"Hello, Pierce?"

He recognized Stacy's voice.

"You wanted to talk to me?"

"Where are you?"

"Trying to find Susan Li."

"I know that, but where are you now?"

"I'm in Oakland. What's it matter?"

"I need to talk to you."

"So, talk."

"Not on the phone. I need to see you."

"Okay, I'll be back in the City in about an hour. Let's meet back in the park by the carousel."

"No, I'll meet you at Magnolia Thunderpussy's. You know where it is?"

"Yeah, Haight and Masonic. See you in an hour," he said and hung up.

He didn't want to ask her over the phone how she got O'Callaghan's number to get hold of him. He wanted to see her expression when he asked.

He smiled at the thought of her sitting in Magnolia Thunderpussy's eating one of its famous erotic desserts while waiting for him. He wondered how long she would wait.

He then dialed the number that Susan Li had left with O'Callaghan. She picked up as soon as the phone rang.

"Hello, Frank?"

"You shouldn't use my name in case anyone is listening," he said.

"I'm sorry, darling, but I've been so anxious. I'll be more careful, I promise."

She sounded too sweet, too nice.

"Where are you?"

"I'm staying with a friend, but I need to see you."

"Okay, but we've got to be careful. The cops are looking for you. Do you know Nick's Rockaway in Pacifica?"

"The place is pretty famous."

"Make sure you're not followed. Then, get a taxi, and I'll meet you in an hour. Bring some clothes, you might not be home for a while."

"In an hour. I'll be there."

"Be careful," he said and heard the phone click in his ear.

CHAPTER TEN

Pierce drove to Nick's straight away and parked in an inconspicuous spot in the parking lot where he could see if she came alone or if she was followed.

Sitting in the van, engulfed in ocean fog, reminded him of the stakeout on Thursday night that started everything.

I've got to get a heavy coat or blankets if I'm going to stay in this racket, he thought.

At exactly one hour, a taxi pulled up at Nick's. Susan Li stepped out carrying a large purse along with a small suitcase and entered the restaurant. Pierce sat in the van and waited. Ten minutes passed before he was satisfied that she hadn't been followed. He found her at the bar nursing a Gibson. She was wearing her sunglasses.

"Beefeater, dry?" he said when he approached her.

"And a Jameson for you?"

"Not tonight," he said as he threw a few dollars on the bar. "Finish your drink. We're leaving."

She finished her Gibson in one swallow, grabbed her large purse, and gets up from her seat.

"Just when I was getting to like it here. Where are we going?" she asked.

"You'll see," he said, picked up her suitcase, and took her by the elbow as they walked out.

Pierce frequently checked the rearview mirror as they drove down to Montara. They spoke little. He needed to know what had happened when he left her in his apartment, that and a number of other things. But he needed her to feel comfortable and safe in the beach house when he asked questions.

By the time they got back to the cabin, the fire had died down with but embers remaining. He added more wood and stirred the fire. It soon blossomed into flame.

"It'll be warm in a minute," he said.

He went to the hall closet and took down a couple of wool blankets and threw them on the couch.

"These'll keep the chill off until the fire builds."

"Cozy," she said.

"I'll get us some drinks. Still Beefeater?"

"That'll be fine. Where's the bathroom?" she asked.

"Down the hall, first door on the right."

He went into the kitchen, shuffled around in a cupboard, and opened the refrigerator.

"I can't find any cocktail onions, only some olives. Will that do?"

He heard no reply. He called to her again, but got no answer. He went to the bathroom door and knocked.

"Are you okay?" he asked.

"I'm fine. I'll be out in a minute," she said.

He returned to the kitchen, mixed a Martini and poured himself a Jameson. When he returned to the front room, she was on the couch huddled under one of the blankets. She had taken off her sunglasses. Her green eyes reflected the orange flames from the fire. He handed her the

The Kiss of the Dragon Lady

Martini. When she took the glass, her blanket fell open revealing that she was naked underneath.

She took a sip from her Martini and put the glass down on the coffee table. He put his glass down next to hers, bent over, and kissed her.

"Make love to me," she said.

He straightened up and took off his jacket. As he unbuttoned his shirt, she unbuckled his belt and undid his pants, letting them fall to floor.

Afterwards, the fire cast a warm glow on their entangled bodies as they lay on the couch. He caressed her hair and kissed her gently.

"I love you," she whispered.

He knew she was lying, but he didn't care. He would pretend it was true if only for a little while longer.

"I know," he said.

The fire burned down. Pierce got up, stirred the embers, and put more wood on the fire. Then, he returned to her outstretched arms.

"Oh, darling, it's so wonderful to be here with you," she said and snuggled closer.

"Yes, it is lovely, isn't it."

Covered in a soft wool blanket, they fell asleep in front of the fire until the wee hours of the morning. When he woke, all that remained of the fire was a tiny glow. He stood, picked her up and carried her to the bedroom. He placed her gently in the bed and covered her with a white down comforter. He got in bed and held her in his arms and fell back to sleep.

He was awakened by the morning sunshine streaming through the bedroom window. He reached for her, but she was not there. He sprang from the bed and called her

H.L. Slater

name. Then he heard the sound of running water.

"I'm taking a shower," she called from the bathroom.

He found a blue, tattered terrycloth robe in the bedroom closet, went to the kitchen, and started coffee. He was sitting at the small kitchen table sipping on his coffee when he heard the bathroom door close. He went to the bedroom and found her sitting on the bed in a black, silk robe.

"Get dressed while I take a shower," he said. "I'll make us something to eat after I get out."

"That sounds lovely. I'm starving."

He went to the bathroom and turned on the water in the shower. He wasn't afraid that she would disappear again, her beauty paraphernalia was spread out next to the sink basin. Seeing it, the memory of Rene momentarily flashed through his head. He dismissed it. When the water was warm, he dropped the robe on the floor, and stepped under the warm water.

After a minute, the shower curtain drew back. She stepped under the water. The shower was small, barely big enough for the both of them. She washed him, their soapy bodies rubbing against each other. He held her close, kissing her as the water cascaded over them.

The shower turned cold.

"We're running out of hot water," he said and shut off the faucet.

They stepped from the shower and dried one another. He drew her close and kissed her.

"Let's go back to bed," he said.

Later, after he made a breakfast of scrambled eggs and bacon, they sat on the rear deck of the beach house drinking coffee and looking at the ocean as the fog

The Kiss of the Dragon Lady

retreated. Her sunglasses were once again in place.

"We have to talk," he said.

"I hate that expression. Nothing ever good happens after someone says,'We have to talk.'"

"Maybe not, but I need to know some things if I'm going to get us out of this jam."

"All right, if we must."

He took a drink of coffee.

"What happened after I left you in my apartment?"

Susan Li takes a deep breath and slowly exhales.

"I was scared," she said. "Right after you left, there was a knock on the door. I didn't answer it, like you told me. But the man knocked again and said he was the police. Then he tried the doorknob. I heard scraping. I think he was trying to pick the lock. I grabbed my shoes and clothes and slid out the back door and down the back stairs and got dressed."

"Got dressed?"

"I was only in my panties. I didn't have time for anything else."

"Then what?"

"I didn't know where you went, so I hailed a taxi and went to a friend's place."

"You found a taxi at that hour?"

"I guess I was lucky."

"And who is this friend?"

"Nobody you know. She doesn't have anything to do with this."

"This friend wouldn't happen to live on Telegraph Hill, would she?"

She looked down. Pierce could see her pulse quicken at her neck.

"No, she lives in Chinatown."

Pierce paused and took another drink of coffee.

"And what about my gun?"

She looked up.

"What about it?"

"I left in on the nightstand when I went out, remember?"

"Yes, but I never touched it."

"It's missing."

She paused for a moment.

"Maybe that cop took it."

Pierce thought for a moment. Maybe Flaherty did take it, but that wouldn't explain how it ended up in Marcia Chow's cottage next to her body. Unless, Flaherty was trying to set him up, but Flaherty was his old partner and covered for him back when the shit hit the fan, and Flaherty couldn't know anything about Marcia Chow. Maybe Flaherty gave the gun to Delaney. They are partners, after all. Then again, maybe it wasn't his gun at Marcia Chow's in the first place. Smith & Wesson .38s are common, and they all look pretty much alike.

Pierce left Susan Li safely tucked away in the Montara beach house and drove up the Coast Highway toward the City. He stopped at the grocery store in Linda Mar and called Stacy Williams. This time Stacy answered the phone.

"Hello."

"It's Frank Pierce."

"Where have you been? Why didn't you meet me?"

"Sorry, I got tied up."

"Did you find her?"

"I'm working on it."

"I told you yesterday that I needed to see you."

The Kiss of the Dragon Lady

"What's so important?"

"I'll tell you when I meet you."

"Okay, in an hour, no, make it two. Same place as yesterday?"

"That place isn't cool any more. Full of tourists. Meet me in front of Park Bowl on Haight."

"Okay," he said before hanging up.

Pierce checked his watch. It was nearly five o'clock. After breakfast, he and Susan Li had spent the day over coffee, conversation, and a few return visits to the bedroom.

He wasn't much for pillow talk, but he learned that Susan Li was born in Canton before the war, and like Dr. Chow, was educated in a missionary school. When Mao Tse-tung and the Communists seized power in 1949, she escaped to Hong Kong where she met and was mentored by Dr. Chow. Under the sponsorship of Marcus Williams, she immigrated to The United States where she tested into UCLA. There, she earned a Bachelor's Degree in Economics and then went on to earn a Master's in Business at Stanford. While a graduate student, she worked for Marcus Williams as his personal assistant that in turn led to an executive position at Williams & Chow after her graduation. She kept in close touch with her mentor and had returned to Hong Kong to visit him on several occasions.

When Pierce asked about what she did at Williams & Chow, she was vague, talking in general terms about managing government importing regulations, invoices, bills of lading, and things of that nature.

In the Haight Ashbury, Pierce found a place to park on

Fell Street. He put his gun and holster behind a loose door panel next to the driver's seat, took off his jacket, threw it across the front seat, crossed the Panhandle, and walked up Clayton Street to Haight. He looked into the window of a secondhand store and decided he needed to change his appearance to try to fit in at least a little. He bought an old Army fatigue jacket and a gray Irish cap. In a head shop, he bought some cheap sunglasses with rose-colored lenses. He was sure he looked like a guy who was trying to be cool, but wasn't.

He hung out in a doorway across from the bowling alley for twenty minutes before Stacy showed up in her buckskin jacket, jeans, and headband. He crossed Haight and came up behind her.

"Stacy."

She turned but at first didn't recognize him in his glasses with his cap pulled down over his face.

"Pierce?"

"You were expecting somebody else?"

"Pierce, you look like crap. Where'd you get that rag you're wearing? You supposed to be in disguise or something?"

He shrugged his shoulders.

"Yeah, I guess. The cops are looking for me."

"Let's go," she said motioning him to follow her.

They walked down Haight, turned down Cole to Oak Street, and rounded the corner. In the middle of the block they climbed the front steps to the stoop of a three-story building, once an elegant Victorian, cut up into several small apartments for later generations of working class men and women and now for their runaway children.

They entered the unlocked door to the right and climbed two floors to the top of the stairs. Stacy's place

The Kiss of the Dragon Lady

was decorated in typical hippie chic including a beanbag chair, a hatch-cover table, and a large waterbed.

Psychedelic posters from the Fillmore Auditorium and other venues featuring The Jefferson Airplane, Big Brother and the Holding Company, and the Grateful Dead, among others were held to the walls with thumbtacks. A hanging lamp covered with a Japanese shade hung from the ceiling. Two thick candles and a glass bong sat on the table next to a copy of Aldous Huxley's *Doors of Perception*.

For a rich girl, Stacy Williams didn't live like one. The only exception was a state-of-the-art stereo system including twin KLH speakers hung on the walls at either side of bay windows that looked out over the Park Panhandle. On either side of the system, LP albums stood on edge, leaning against the walls.

"Where's your roommate?" he asked.

"I don't have a roommate," she said.

"You live here alone?"

"Sometimes, sometimes not. Make yourself at home," she said indicating the beanbag. "I'll be back in a minute."

He sat, or more accurately fell, into the beanbag. When she returned, she had removed her jacket. She was wearing a tie-dye T-shirt. Underneath, it was obvious she wasn't wearing a bra.

"So, what is so urgent that you couldn't tell me over the telephone?" he asked.

"We can get to that in a minute."

She knelt down beside the low table and took out a small metal tin. She filled the bong with a small piece of hashish, lit it and inhaled, and then offered it to Pierce.

He shook his head.

"Maybe later, after we finish our business."

"Suit yourself," she said and then lit the candles and took another long hit from the bong.

"I'm hungry," she said and jumped up.

She walked down a short hallway to where Pierce figured was a kitchen. After a few minutes, she brought back a bottle of Chianti wrapped in straw, two water glasses, and a few wafers on a small plate. She poured the wine and handed a glass to Pierce and offered him the plate of wafers. They reminded him of Holy Communion. "The Body of Christ" the priest would say as he placed a wafer on Pierce's tongue back in the days when he still went to church.

He ate one.

Shit! He realized that it was a communion wafer and washed it down with a gulp of Chianti.

"So now that you got me alone, what is it that you wanted so desperately to talk to me about?" he asked.

She plopped down on the bare wood floor, crossed her legs underneath her, and put on a cute little girl smile.

"What's your hurry, Mr. Pierce? Don't you like me?"

He could see that he wasn't going to get anywhere without humoring her. He drank a little more Chianti.

"Of course, I like you. You're a bright, charming girl."

She took another hit from the bong.

"That's not what I mean, Frank. I hope you don't mind if I call you Frank?"

"Frank's fine."

"When I was down at Stanford, I met a professor who was a lot like you."

"Yeah, how so?"

"He was real intense and kind of shy. You know, a real square but cute at the same time. I let him fuck me. Would you like to fuck me, Frank?"

The Kiss of the Dragon Lady

Pierce was silent.

"You think I'm kidding? I think you're kind of cute...for an old guy."

"I'm flattered. But there's rules about sleeping with someone who's paying you. And you are my client, remember."

"Just like the rules about teachers sleeping with their students."

"Something like that."

He looked at Stacy. She sat on the floor looking up at him with that weird little girl smile on her face. Stacy was cute, real cute in that hippie girl sort of way.

What the fuck was going on? Her face became a mask, at first beautiful, but then distorted, grotesque. Her hair was bright green, no red. The room swirled around. He HEARD MUSIC. COLORS danced around the room. Stacy dancing. *...anybody find me somebody to...* Where's Stacy? Who's dancing? *...got no common sense...*

B l u e ,   o r a n g e , purple. ...moving...moving...moving *...ooh, somebody to love...* Pierce heard his own voice from far away. No, no, no... Help me! He saw Susan Li's green eyes staring at him. ...falling, falling, falling...

She smelled like lilacs...

CHAPTER ELEVEN

Pierce didn't know where he was. Strong sunlight coming through the bay windows gave him no clue until he saw the psychedelic posters covering the walls. He rolled over and felt the slosh of the waterbed. Stacy was curled up beside him in a fetal position. They were both naked.

So much for rules about client relations, he thought. Oh well, they were only guidelines anyway.

He had a desperate need to urinate and tried without success to get up without sending waves rippling across the bed.

He found the bathroom down the hall. When he returned, he gathered up his clothes, from where they were scattered around the floor, and got dressed. His first inclination was to tiptoe out of the apartment, but he had to find out why she was so desperate to see him. Or was it just for a quick roll in the hay. No, it was more than that, he was sure. Her voice over the phone had sounded urgent.

He sat on the waterbed causing it to bob up and down and shook Stacy by the shoulder. She raised her head and looked at him through halfway closed eyes.

"Good morning," he said. "Do you have anything to eat around here? I'm starving."

"There's some coffee and bagels in the kitchen pantry," she said and fell back into her pillow.

Pierce went into the kitchen. When he returned with a couple of cups of coffee and two toasted bagels, Stacy was sitting up in bed.

"I couldn't find any cream or sugar, and I hope you like your bagels with just plain butter," he said as he placed a plate with the bagels and two cups of coffee on the table.

"You'll make someone a good wife, Frank," she said.

She got out of bed and walked to the bathroom. When she returned, she was wearing a short, silk robe that she left open.

"What was that you slipped me? LSD?" he asked. "I remember music and lights. We were dancing, right? Or did I just imagine it?"

"Yeah, we were grooving pretty good, before you tripped out."

"Tripped out?"

"Don't worry, you didn't do anything weird, at least not too weird."

Pierce picks up his coffee, takes a sip, and returns the cup to the table.

"Did we... have sex?"

"Have sex? God, you are old, Frank. No, we didn't fuck. You couldn't get it up. Kept talking about lilacs, or some shit like that."

Pierce didn't know whether to be relieved or embarrassed.

"I'm sorry if..."

"No worries. Happens sometimes when you're trippin'.

We'll fix it next time."

Stacy took a bite out of one of the bagels and drank some coffee.

"I told you Su-Li killed my father. Now I've got proof."

"Proof? What kind of proof? What do you know about Susan Li?"

"Her name isn't Susan Li. It's Chow Su-Li. She's Dr. Chow's daughter."

Pierce took a moment to consider what Stacy said.

"That's maybe so, but that doesn't prove that she had anything to do with killing your father."

"I heard them arguing the same day after he hired you."

"I know. You told me that already."

"Not everything," she said and took another drink of coffee. "You don't happen to have a cigarette by any chance?"

"I don't smoke, remember."

"Yeah, neither do I."

"Go on with what you were telling me," he said.

Stacy paused, took a bite out of a bagel, and drank some coffee.

"My father and Paul Chow were smugglers," Stacy said.

Pierce wasn't surprised. He had suspected that something shady was going on other than theft from the warehouse.

"What were Susan Li, ...er, Su-Li, and your father arguing about?"

"She accused my father of having Dr. Chow murdered."

"Murdered? Are you telling me that Dr. Chow is dead?"

"His body was found in his apartment in Hong Kong. The police report said it looked like the work of a Triad."

The Kiss of the Dragon Lady

The thought of a Chinese Triad sent chills down Pierce's spine. Common knowledge was that a Hong Kong Triad was closely connected to the Tongs of San Francisco's Chinatown. And although the powerful Triads of mainland China had great influence in the world's cities with large Chinese immigrant communities, they rarely, if ever, interfered in each other's spheres of influence. The Triads' strict organizational boundaries made the Mafia's look amateurish in comparison.

If Dr. Chow's and, by extension, Marcus Williams's killings were connected, signaling the first salvo of a dispute between rival Triads, Pierce wanted nothing to do with it. If on the other hand, he couldn't find a way of extricating himself, he would certainly play the fall guy for at least the Williams killing. The best he could hope for would be to spend the rest of his life in San Quentin in a small room without a view, or the worst, his body would be fished out of San Francisco Bay.

"What were they smuggling?" Pierce asked.

"I don't know for certain, but I think it was opium."

"Why do you think that?"

"I grew up in my father's house. People coming and going at all hours, most of them Chinese. People talk. You overhear things."

"So you think Susan..., Su-Li, killed your father for revenge for her father's murder? That doesn't make sense."

"No, she killed my father on the orders of the Chinese Tongs here in the City. I heard her warn him that would happen if he didn't cooperate."

"What did she mean by 'cooperate?'"

"I don't know. But I know she had important connections in Chinatown. Everywhere she went, everyone treated her as someone important, someone to be feared."

"That still doesn't prove she killed your father. It easily could've been someone else."

"Whoever it was had to be someone close to him. Yan-ling was not only our butler, but my father's bodyguard. He wouldn't let anyone near him that he didn't know. And my father had police protection. He was a Police Commissioner, after all."

"Don't remind me. How about the butler? The butler always did it in the old movies."

"Yan-ling was my father's friend since they fought together in China during the War. He would never betray my father, never, I know it."

"Judas did it for thirty pieces of silver. I'm sure smuggling opium pays much better."

"Find Su-Li. The cops will make her talk."

Pierce said nothing. He knew she was right.

It was still morning when Pierce left Stacy's apartment. His first thought was to drive back to Montara and confront Susan Li, Su-Li, or whatever her name was, and make her tell him what the fuck was going on. But on second thought, he decided to do a little digging on his own. He went to the pay phone in front of the bowling alley, found a dime in his pocket, and called O'Callaghan's.

"Mickey, it's me. Did anyone call?"

"Who the hell is this?"

"Your driver."

"Yeah, your old lady called and asked me to tell you she's pregnant."

"Is she all right?"

"I don't know. She called just before closing last night

looking for you. I told her I hadn't seen you. Don't worry. I covered for you. Told her you're just an old tomcat out on the prowl. Haven't heard from her since."

"With friends like you, a guy don't need enemies. Is that all?"

"Your old pals came back looking for you. I gave 'em the same story."

Mickey's voice showed concerned.

"They want you bad. You better be real careful."

Pierce hung up the phone, dropped another dime in the slot, and called the Montara number. He let it ring, but no one answered.

Damn, he thought, she's probably afraid to pick up. I should've set up a signal, so she'd know that it was me calling.

He hung up and heard the dime fall into the return slot, picked it up, and dialed another number, one he knew by heart. The phone rang several times before he heard a sleepy voice on the other end of the line.

"Yeah, who's this?"

"Pierce."

"Pierce? ...Frank Pierce?"

"Benny, I need your help."

"I can't help you. You're hotter than a firecracker on Chinese New Year," Benny Quan said.

"I know I can't show my face in Chinatown, but I have nowhere else to turn. My ass is on the line."

"If anyone found out I'm talking to you, my ass would be hung out to dry just like yours. The word is that you iced that big prick, Williams."

"I'm being set up, Benny. I had nothing to do with it. I need some information, fast, or I'm dead, and you know everything that goes on in Chinatown."

There was a long silence at the other end of the phone.

"Meet me at the old place. Wear a hat," Benny Quan said and hung up.

Pierce took forty-five minutes to drive to Aquatic Park on the waterfront, find a place to leave the van, and walk halfway out on the Muni Pier where a fisherman was dangling his line in the murky waters of the Bay.

"How are they biting?"

"Better if I'd bothered to bait the hook," Benny Quan said.

Benny Quan was wearing an old pair of khakis and a weathered plaid flannel shirt. A well-worn bucket hat, with assorted lures attached, completed the picture.

"It's been awhile. How've you been, Benny?"

"No need to apologize, Pierce. I know you're a *persona non grata* in Chinatown. But you didn't reach out to me for old times' sake. What can I do for you?"

"You got to know, I didn't kill Williams. I was working for him on a small case, sure. But it was nothing serious, just some..."

Benny held up his hand.

"I don't need to know anything. I don't want to know anything that has to do with Williams. He's dead and the world's a better place for it."

"Yeah, I'm getting that feeling more and more. What do you know about opium smuggling in Chinatown?"

Benny Quan sighed.

"Haven't you learned your lesson, Pierce? You worked Chinatown when you were a cop.

"You've gotten yourself into a big pile of shit. Nobody, and I mean nobody, wants anyone sniffing around Chinatown when it comes to drugs. Smoking opium has long been a part of Chinese culture, and when my people first came here over a hundred years ago, they brought their culture with them just like the Italians or the Irish."

"I don't care if anyone wants to get high in Chinatown. I just need to get myself out from under a murder rap. But to do that, I got to know why Williams was killed, and I think it had to do with drugs."

Benny Quan was silent for several minutes as if in deep thought.

"You're probably right. Maybe Williams's death had to do with drugs, but not in the way you might think. Today, things aren't the same. The days of old men smoking opium in some dingy basement are long gone. Kids from across the country are flooding in here in answer to that fucking song, *"if you are going to San Francisco, wear some flowers in your hair,"* or some such crap. It might all be love, love, love now, but the vultures are circling."

"How so? The hippies seem pretty harmless to me."

"They're not the problem. Everybody feeding off of their naivety, that's the problem. 'Turn on, tune in, drop out' might sound like an answer in a world turned to shit, but things are only going to get worse."

"You sound like a philosopher, Benny."

"Every bartender is a philosopher, Pierce, if you want to survive all the crap people give you."

"Maybe you're right, but what does that have to do with my problem?"

"Pot and hash may be popular, but heroin use is skyrocketing. There's millions to be made overnight, and there's a war going on over who's going to control the flow of narcotics coming into the country. Looks like you've been caught in the middle of it."

"Why me? I never had anything to do with narcotics. I

worked vice."

"I don't rightly know, but you have a reputation of being a dirty cop. Maybe that had something to do with it."

"You know better than that, Quan. My problem was that I wasn't a dirty cop."

"Sure, I think you got a raw deal, or else I wouldn't be here sticking my neck out talking to you like this."

"So, Williams and his partner were big players in smuggling drugs."

"When you make your living walking the plank behind the bar, you see things, hear things. But you also learn to become deaf, dumb, and blind if you want to stay gainfully employed..., and healthy. So, you didn't hear anything from me, got it?

"This is a lot bigger than Williams and his supposed war buddy. They were more or less a mom and pop operation. They were the importers of a lot more than junk shop trinkets. They were agents for a Triad in Hong Kong and the Tongs here. They brought in opium for local use, but then they decided to branch out and ship heroin. That stepped on the toes of another Triad in mainland China, and to make matters worse, the Mafia and some Mexican gangs expressed interest in the growing trade.

"The word on the street is that Williams and his partner were being squeezed out and didn't look too kindly at the changing world order," Benny Quan said.

"But that still doesn't tell me why Williams was killed or who's responsible."

"I told you all I know. The rest you'll have to dig out for yourself."

"Thanks, I'm no closer to finding out by who or why I was set up, but at least I know what park I'm playing in.

The Kiss of the Dragon Lady

"I've got one more question," Pierce said. "What do you know about Susan Li?"

Benny Quan looked Pierce right in the eye before he spoke.

"The Dragon Lady? You already have enough trouble for a dumb Harp, my friend, but if you are tied up with her, you really are fucked."

Pierce felt uneasy. He hoped that he wouldn't learn anything more damning about Susan Li than he had heard from Stacy.

"How do you mean that?"

"She's the most beautiful women I ever met. But she's poison."

"What do you know about her?"

"Nothing, really. I've met her, of course, but I know her only by reputation."

"Go on," Pierce said.

"Everywhere she goes, she is treated with deference. If these were the old days, I think people in Chinatown would actually kowtow to her. The rumor has it that she is connected not only to the local Tongs but to the Triads in mainland China as well."

"How do you mean, 'connected?'"

"She's an expediter, a trouble shooter. Gets things done. You know what I mean."

"What things?"

"Jeez, Pierce, What kind of cop were you? Do I have to spell it out to you? She does what needs to be done."

"Including murder?"

"Hey, I didn't say that. I told you I don't know her that well. Besides, if you're talking about Williams, that would be crazy. He was her connection into the Police Department and City Hall. At least that's the word on the street."

"Paul Chow was found dead in Hong Kong. The police think one of the Triads is responsible."

"Yeah, I heard."

"Not much gets by you, does it, Benny?"

"I hear things."

"Would it surprise you to learn that Susan Li is really Paul Chow's daughter?"

Benny Quan grinned.

"You really are walking around with your head up your ass, Pierce. Susan Li isn't Chow's daughter, the other one was," he said.

"Other one?"

"Yeah, the one that works in Williams's office. I don't remember her first name, ...Maggie..., Mary..."

"Marcia."

"Yeah, that's it, Marcia. You want to learn something, talk to her."

"She's dead," Pierce said.

"When?"

"Three days ago. Guess your rumor pipeline is getting plugged up."

Benny Quan was silent for a moment.

"Maybe so, or more likely the cops are sitting on it. Find out why, and you'll find some answers," Benny Quan said.

CHAPTER TWELVE

Pierce found a payphone near the entrance to Aquatic Park and called the Montara number, still no answer. He checked his watch, ten minutes after four. Even with afternoon traffic leaving the City, it should take him less than an hour to drive to the beach house. When he got to the van, he found a ticket on the windshield. He looked at the red and white street sign: Tow-Away Zone, 4 p.m. to 6 p.m., Weekdays.

Shit! Well, at least I beat the tow truck. That's the only good thing that's happened today, he thought.

The sun slipped toward the afternoon fog hanging on the ocean as he drove down the Coast Highway. At the cabin, he listened a moment at the front door for any sound from within, then tried the doorknob but found it locked as he expected.

He knocked, and called out, "Susan, it's me."

He waited. No reply. He knocked again.

"Susan, if you're in there, open the door."

Still no reply.

He walked around the house to the rear and climbed the

few steps to the back deck. The rear door was unlocked. He went in.

"Susan, are you all right?"

Searching the beach house didn't take long, but he didn't find her.

Fuck! he thought. Where could she have gone? She doesn't have a car. She could've caught a taxi or even a bus, but where in the hell would she go?

Just then, he heard the door from the back deck open. He instinctively reached for his gun, but he had left it in the van. He turned to see Susan Li in the doorway silhouetted against the setting sun.

"I was afraid you had left," he said.

"I was worried sick when you didn't return. I was afraid the police had picked you up, or worse," she said.

"I'm sorry. I called several times but you didn't pick up."

"I heard the phone ring, but I didn't want to take a chance of anyone else knowing where I am."

"If I have to leave again, I'll call and let the phone ring three times, hang up, and call back right away."

"You're leaving again?"

"I'll probably have to if we're going to get out of this jam. But not tonight," he said and took her into his arms and held her close as they kissed.

Later, after a light supper of a cheese and spinach frittata, helped along with glasses of Chardonnay, he built a fire to ward off the chill of the ocean fog that by now had engulfed the beach house once again. As they sat in front of the fire nursing what remained of their wine, she removed her sunglasses and snuggled close to him. The flames danced in her green eyes. At that moment, he didn't care if she was a drug smuggler, didn't care if she had killed Williams, didn't care about anything except saving her, saving her for himself.

But to do that, he had to risk everything.

"If we're going to get free of all of this, you've got to talk to me."

Susan Li sat up and took a drink of the wine.

"I mean it," he said. "I don't care what you've done in the past. That's all over now. You told me to never let go. Well, I'm not letting go, not now, not ever, but I've got to know everything, or we'll both be looking at the world from behind bars, that's if we're lucky."

"I could use a little more wine, or better something stronger," she said.

He went into the kitchen and returned with a Martini. He set it down on the coffee table and sat down beside her. She took the drink and swallowed it before returning the glass to the table.

"Aren't you having anything?" she asked.

"Maybe later."

She looked at him with tears welling up in her green eyes.

"I don't know where to begin," she said.

"Let's start with why I was hired for that bogus watchdog routine."

"I was against it. I want you to know that. It was Marcus's, ...er, Mr. Williams's idea. He thought if anyone was going to steal the shipment, knowing the place was being watched would scare them off long enough to get the merchandise out of the warehouse."

"He must've had plenty of people who could've done that for him. Why hire me?"

"He didn't know who he could trust. I don't think he

even trusted me. He wanted somebody that didn't have a stake in the game. And he needed someone who was expendable if things went badly."

Pierce thought for several moments.

"That's bullshit, and you know it. Whatever was in that warehouse was gone well before I was hired. I was a decoy so anyone interested would think the 'merchandise' was still inside. Opium, isn't that right? Wasn't it opium, Su-Li?"

She looked up at the mention of her name and nodded.

"And other things."

"Other things?"

She picked up her glass from the table and discovered that she had emptied it.

"If I must tell you everything, I think I've earned a refill," she said and handed her glass to Pierce.

He went into the kitchen and returned with a fresh Martini and handed it to her.

"Go easy, darling. I don't want you comatose. I need your story straight if I'm going to get us out of this mess."

He sat back down on the couch and took her hand.

"I promised I wouldn't let you go, no matter what, and I meant it. What else was Williams smuggling?"

She took a drink and continued.

"Gold," she said.

"Gold? Why gold? That sounds like something out of the last century."

"Even before Japan invaded or the Communists seized power, rich Chinese were converting their wealth to gold and burying it, so it wouldn't be confiscated.

Most of the gold that is smuggled out of China goes through Hong Kong, with the Triads acting as agents in dealing with corrupt officials in both mainland China and Hong Kong. This arrangement works for everybody's benefit. Everybody gets a slice of the pie, but the bulk of smuggled gold gets to immigrant family members around the world. If it didn't, the trade would dry up, and the Triads know it."

"So, what happened to change things?"

She took another drink of the Martini.

"Most of the gold amassed by the Chinese ruling classes over centuries of famine and poverty remains buried in China. But the trickle of gold from China is increasing. As we get closer to 1997, it will become a flood."

"1997, that's when the British return Hong Kong to China, right?"

"Looks like somebody paid attention in History class."

"I read about Hong Kong in Time Magazine."

The second Martini was taking effect. Susan Li was more relaxed. She still was careful with her words, but she was more open.

"Gold is pretty heavy. How does..., how did Williams get it into the country without raising suspicion?" Pierce asked.

"Well, he had connections on the waterfront and at City Hall as well as inside the Police Department. Money changed hands, what else can I say."

"That I can figure, but wouldn't shipping bars of gold be too risky?"

"Have you ever noticed red dragons in the shops along Grant Avenue? They're made of cast iron, painted with red lacquer?"

"I seem to recall them, about a foot tall."

"That's right. Except some that were shipped are not

made of cast iron."

"Clever."

"They are copies of a real ancient artifact from the Han Dynasty. The original is made of gold and painted in red lacquer. But the dragon's eyes are rubies, and the scales are emeralds and sapphires. The Han Dragon was a favorite of Cixi, the Dowager Empress."

Susan Li's eyes widened and looked away as she spoke of the Han Dragon.

"What do you think it's worth, in dollars, I mean?"

"I wouldn't have the slightest idea. It's priceless. Worth more than 'all the tea in China' as the saying goes."

"Where is it now?"

"No one knows. It disappeared. It's rumored that it was last seen in the shop of a dealer in ancient artifacts in Hong Kong in 1949. But if that's true, it was probably a fake anyway. My guess is that it's buried like the rest of China's treasures."

"Probably, but it makes you wonder, forbidden gold, ancient legends..." he said.

"Frank, at heart you are a true romantic, not a hardboiled detective like you profess."

"Guilty, I'm afraid. But every Irishman's a poet at heart, so I have an excuse."

He paused for a moment, then continued, "It's getting late, let's get back to the business at hand. How about heroin? Was that brought in, too?"

"You're right. It is getting late. Let's go to bed."

They fell asleep in each other's arms, but Pierce spent a restless night dreaming of gold dragons and Susan Li. Her face smiled at him then she morphed into a Chinese dragon painted red and gold. Then he saw her in her long, black robe walking up a dark forest path toward sunlight ahead. He chased after her but couldn't catch her.

As he awoke, he felt her arms around him, her warm body against his back. It was still early, the first rays of dawn filtered through shuttered windows. He turned over and stared at her sleeping face. The faint smell of lilac *eau de toilette* filled his nose. Gently he kissed her cheek. She opened her eyes and smiled. Without a word, she rolled on top of him, and they made love. Afterwards, she cuddled in his arms.

"I love you," she whispered.

If only that were true, he thought before he fell back to sleep.

When they woke, the sun was high in the sky, the morning fog in retreat. After a light breakfast of coffee and muffins, they walked hand in hand on the beach. At first they spoke little, each enjoying the nearness of the other.

"I need to tell you about the heroin," she said.

"Yes, you do, but I didn't want to break the spell of a perfect morning."

They sat on an old piece of driftwood, washed high up on the beach in a violent storm. She pulled her black cardigan together around her shoulders.

"Are you cold?" he asked.

"No, I'm fine."

He hadn't wanted to begin the conversation. He was grateful she broached the subject.

"Last night you asked about heroin. Competition from the Mafia and Mexico threatened the near monopoly of the Triads in Chinese communities around the world. But now, the demand for heroin has increased dramatically outside just the world's Chinatowns. So, yes, to answer your question, heroin along with the traditional opium was shipped from Hong Kong."

"Your boss, Williams, seemed to be pretty well connected with the powers that be in San Francisco with a nice import-export business. Why did he get mixed up with drugs?"

"Let's walk some more," she said and got to her feet.

Pierce followed, and they resumed their stroll through the sand.

"Did he tell you about his exploits in China during the war?"

"About being in the Flying Tigers and getting wounded? Yeah, he told me the story."

"He told it to anyone who would listen. And guess what. It's all true..., as far as it goes."

"There's more?"

"Well, as you might guess, everything was in short supply during the war, especially medical supplies. Morphine and other painkillers were nearly nonexistent except on the black market. Fortunately, or maybe not so fortunately, Paul Chow was well acquainted with men who smuggled opium from India to sell in China, so he was able to get what he needed for his patients in the base infirmary."

"That sounds like a good thing to me."

"Marcus Williams, like many others, became addicted to the drug."

"I see, so he had it shipped home to feed his habit."

"It might have started that way, but that was later. He was stuck in China and continued to fight with the Kuomintang against the Japanese until the end of the war. By that time, he and Paul Chow were great friends, so they decided to form an import-export business together. At first, they just exported inexpensive, toys and knickknacks—finger traps, bamboo back scratchers, small laughing Buddhas—things like that, but they quickly discovered that they could hide the white powder in the shipments without trouble.

"Williams came from an influential family with important political connections, so when he imported Chinese novelties, no one looked too closely."

"That's all very interesting, but how are you involved?"

Susan Li took a few more steps before stopping and turning to face Pierce.

"As you can imagine, there can be a lot of pitfalls in smuggling contraband. My job was to see that everything ran smoothly. I am, was, the front person for Williams & Chow. Williams kept to the background as much as possible, so I had to deal with the everyday workings of the company. I know where the bodies are buried so to speak."

"That doesn't narrow down who's trying to keep you quiet. Sounds like a lot of people would be better off if you disappeared..., and drop a poison pellet on me for that, too."

CHAPTER THIRTEEN

They walked back up the beach without speaking. As they neared the cabin, Susan Li thought she saw movement inside through a window. She grabbed Pierce and pulled him down behind a sand dune covered with tall sea grass.

"What?"

"I think someone's inside the house," she said.

"What did you see?"

"The light inside changed like someone crossed in front of the window."

"All right, let's get back down the beach where it's safer."

They ducked low until they were out of sight of the cabin, then ran down the beach three hundred yards, and climbed the sand-covered embankment.

"Wait here," he said. "I'll go down the road and see if I can find out if there's anyone there."

"No, I'm going with you. I'm not going to get stuck out here not knowing what's going on if something happens to you."

"All right, but stay behind me."

The Kiss of the Dragon Lady

They moved up to the road and cautiously approached the cabin. No windows from which they could be seen faced that side of the cabin. He looked around but only saw the van parked on the far side. There were no other cars in sight.

Fuck! he thought, why didn't I take the gun?

"What'll we do now? We can't just go up and knock on the door and say, 'Hi, mind if we come in?'" she said.

"That's just what I intend to do. The way I see it, if it's the cops inside, they'll just arrest me. If it's someone else, they want me alive to take the fall for two homicides. And there's another thing. I was a cop, and I still have friends on the force. Cops don't like it when one of their own gets taken out, even one like me. They tend to go blind and shoot first, get what I mean?"

"How can you be so sure?"

"I can't, but if you can think of anything else, I'm listening."

Pierce reached into his pocket, took out the key to the van, and handed it to her.

"Once I'm inside, give me a couple of minutes to distract whoever is in there, then go to the van. My gun is inside the driver's side door panel. All you have to do is pull the panel away from the door, and you'll see it."

"You remember how to fire a Smith & Wesson .38?"

"I'll figure it out," she said.

"I'm sure you will."

"Please don't get yourself killed, darling. I've grown rather fond of you," she said and bent toward him and kissed his cheek.

Pierce stood up, and as casually as he could manage, walked to the front door of the cabin. He was about to knock but thought to try the knob first. The door was unlocked. He opened it slowly and stepped inside leaving the door ajar. Maybe Susan Li was wrong. Maybe the beach house was empty. Then he heard the toilet flush.

His first impulse was to grab something with which to defend himself, but he reconsidered. If the intruder was armed, assailing him would be a good way to get shot. He sat in a chair with his back to the rear of the beach house facing the kitchen, hoping whoever was in the bathroom would come in the room and face him, putting the intruder's back toward the front door.

He heard the door to the bathroom open and close. He watched, his heart pounding, as the intruder entered the room at the same instant as Susan Li burst through the front door, her legs spread at the ready and both hands out in front holding his revolver pointing at Mickey O'Callaghan.

"What the...!" O'Callaghan shouted as he threw his arms in the air.

"Don't shoot! This is my friend, Mickey," Pierce shouted.

"Holy Mother of God. You scared the crap out of me, Pierce. What the hell is going on?"

"You can put your hands down, O'Callaghan. Sorry we scared you, but we didn't know who you were."

O'Callaghan sat down on the couch.

"You got a drink around here for a guy who's got a heart condition?" O'Callaghan asked.

"I'll get you some whiskey. I didn't know you had a bad heart, Mickey."

"I didn't 'till just now."

Susan Li didn't say anything, but kept her eyes on O'Callaghan through her sunglasses as she sat in another chair, the gun resting on a table beside her.

The Kiss of the Dragon Lady

Pierce went to the kitchen and returned with a shot of whiskey, which O'Callaghan knocked back.

When he finished the whiskey, he asked, "Who's your lady friend?"

"Just a friend."

"Well, it looks like your friend knows what she's doing the way she was holding that piece. I was afraid I was a goner for sure."

"What are you doing here, O'Callaghan?"

"I didn't want to call. I was afraid somebody could be listening in, maybe tracing the call. But that old partner of yours came by again asking a lot questions. Then I spotted him in a car across from the bar. I figured he was waiting for you to show up."

"You're sure you weren't followed?"

"I'm sure."

"How'd you get here? I didn't see a car outside."

"I parked up the road about a quarter mile and walked down the beach, just to be sure that no one was on my tail."

Susan Li spoke up for the first time, "We were on the beach. Which way did you come?"

"From the City."

She seemed satisfied as they had walked southward in the morning.

Pierce thought for a moment.

"Mickey, does anybody else know about this place? I mean anybody the cops might question?"

"I doubt it. I inherited it when my old man died. They would have to dig pretty deep, I left his name on the tax records and electric bill, but the phone is in my name."

"I think we're safe here, at least for a while. Thanks, Mickey, but you better get back to the bar before those teamsters break down the door."

"It's okay. I got my brother Tommy to open up for me."

"Still, if the cops are looking at you, you better get back before you're gone too long."

"Another thing, the van's registered in my name. If they asked me where it is, what do you want me to tell 'em?"

"Tell them the truth. You lent it to me last week and haven't seen it since. And if you need to call here, let it ring four times, hang up, and call right back."

"Anything else?"

"Yeah, I'm going to come back up to the City and act as if everything is copasetic. If they want me to lead them on a wild goose chase, I'll oblige them."

After O'Callaghan left, Susan Li went into the bedroom and pulled on a pair of white jeans and a green turtleneck sweater. When she returned, she sat on the arm of the couch.

"I've been thinking. The heroin must still be in the warehouse in the bottom of the crates under the cast iron figures. But the heroin is not what this is about," she said.

"So, what is it about?"

"You were right about Marcus hiring you to be a decoy, but what people were after wasn't opium or heroin. Dr. Chow shipped a set of six gold dragons, each of a different design. They're from the Ming Dynasty and aren't nearly as rare as the Han Dragon, but together as a set could be worth well over a million dollars, maybe more."

"And the heroin, how much is it worth?"

"Less than $100,000, I'd say. Maybe ten times that on the street after it's cut, but Williams was just the importer, not the distributor."

The Kiss of the Dragon Lady

"Well, $100,000 is nothing to sneeze at."

"There was a note written at the top of the shipping order for the cast iron figures that read 'Ross.'"

"Who's Ross?" Pierce asked.

"It's not a who, it's a place, Ross Alley in Chinatown."

"Yeah, I know it. Got quite a history from back in the bad old days, but where in Ross Alley?"

"There's a basement that can only be accessed from a stairway that leads from the street."

"Do you know the address?"

"There isn't any address, at least not one I know of. I've never been there. But it's just a plain door, painted green with some sort of dragon on it. Marcus told me about it after I heard him talking on the phone about shipments, opium I think, that could be stashed there if things got too hot."

"When did you hear this?"

"A few years ago. He wasn't talking about anything to do with this last shipment, but it's the only place I can think of."

"Well, we can't go strolling through Chinatown looking for a door with a dragon, knock, and say 'howdy, we're here to pick up the stolen dragons,'" Pierce said.

"Even if we found it, we couldn't get in without a key. The place is locked up tight with an alarm that must be shut off from inside within thirty seconds of the door opening."

"Where's the key?"

"I know there was a key in the safe at the office, but knowing Marcus he must've had another one at home, probably in his wall safe."

"The safe in the office was empty when I looked inside, so that only leaves the one in Los Altos. You wouldn't happen to know the combination would you?"

"I don't, but I know someone who does."

"Well, don't keep me in suspense."

"Your little playmate, Stacy, that's who."

Did he detect a tone of jealousy in her voice? He had mentioned his encounter with Stacy when Susan Li had asked him about his absence before his return to Montara. She had shown no resentment at the time, but now...

"She's not going to give me the combination if she knows we're together," he said. "I'll call her. Maybe I can set up a meeting."

Susan Li said nothing. She sat down on the couch, her back supported by a pillow, and crossed her arms across her chest.

CHAPTER FOURTEEN

Pierce drove back to the City, parked the van in front of his apartment building, and walked to O'Callaghan's. If anyone was looking for him, he wanted them to know where he was and what he was up to. If he was going to find out who was setting him up, he needed to stir things up a bit.

When he entered O'Callaghan's, six or seven men were drinking at the bar, only two of them he recognized as neighborhood regulars.

"Hey, Mickey, pull me a Guinness. Being a gumshoe is thirsty work," he said loud enough for everyone to hear.

"Where ya been keeping yourself, Pierce? Haven't seen you around for a couple days," O'Callaghan said.

The two of them made small talk for a few minutes. After Pierce finished his drink, he went up to his office and plopped down behind his desk, retrieved Stacy's number from his wallet, and dialed her number. The phone rang several times before the husky voice answered.

"Yeah?"

"This is Frank Pierce. Let me speak to Stacy."

"You're the private dick she told me about. She ain't here."

"When will she be back?"

"How the fuck should I know?"

"Well, do you know where she went?"

"Who the fuck do you think I am? Her fucking social secretary," the girl said and hung up.

Pierce dialed the Montara number, let it ring three times, hung up, and dialed again.

Susan Li picked up immediately and listened without speaking.

"It's me," he said.

"Is everything okay?"

"Yeah, I tried to get hold of Stacy, but she's not home. You think she's down at the Los Altos house after what happened?"

"How should I know? Maybe. She stays there once in a while when she runs out of cash from her trust fund and can't find anyone to sleep with."

"Meow. That doesn't sound like you."

"Sorry, but the little bitch gets under my skin. Her father gave her everything. Sent her to the best private schools and even got her into Stanford. I worked my ass off to get in, and she gets it all gift wrapped with a pretty bow only to fuck around and drop out after the first semester."

Pierce paused until Susan Li finished her tirade.

"What's the phone number of the house?" he asked.

"Got a pen and paper?"

"Shoot."

He wrote the number she gave him on a yellow pad he kept in the top drawer of his desk.

"That's the house's private number," she said. "If she's

there, she'll pick up."

"Thanks, if I get hold of her, I'll go down and see if I can get her to open the safe."

"Be careful," she said, but he had already hung up the phone.

He dialed the number on the yellow pad. After several rings, he recognized Stacy's voice.

"Hello?"

"It's Pierce."

"Where the fuck have you been? I called your office and that shitty saloon you hang out in."

"Simmer down. I've been busy. I found Susan Li."

There was a silence at the other end of the line.

"Hello? Did you hear what I said? I found Su-Li."

"Where is she?"

"I've got her stashed."

"Where?"

"I'll tell you when I see you. I'd like to come down to the house."

"Are you in the City? I can come up to meet you."

"No, I'll come to you."

"All right, how long will you take to get here?"

"Give me an hour, okay?"

"In one hour," she said and hung up.

Pierce took the Healey out of the garage and put the top down. If someone wanted to tail him, he'd make it easy. As he put the little sports car through its paces, the fresh air and sunshine relieved him of much of the apprehension that had plagued him since he heard of Marcus Williams's death.

His only moments of elation had been with Susan Li. The first time he saw her descending the stairs, he felt his blood jump and the old uneasy anxiety rise in his chest. She excited him in a way no other woman had ever done before.

He had loved Rene, still did for whatever it was worth. But his feelings for Susan Li were different—a desire, a compulsion—he had to have her no matter the cost.

Stop thinking that way, he told himself, or you'll find yourself floating face down in the Bay.

Stacy Williams greeted him at the door. She had discarded her hippie garb for a floral-print dress and raised heel sandals. She wore her hair in a French twist. What a chameleon, he thought, if I didn't know better, I would have thought she was someone else entirely.

"Welcome to the mausoleum," she said.

Pierce followed her into the study where he had met her father the week before. He sat in the same chair.

"I'd offer you something to drink," she said, "but it's the servants' decade off."

"You're here alone?"

"Quite alone. If you try to take advantage of me, I hope you do a better job of it than last time."

"I'll try to contain myself," he said.

"You're still working for me, I assume. Let's get down to business. I want to see Su-Li. Where is she?"

"We'll get to that in a minute, but first, why are you so desperate to see her?"

"She killed my father. Do I need another reason?"

"First of all, she didn't kill your father, and I think you know that. Secondly, if you really believed she was the killer, you could just tell the police where she could be found. You'd have no need to see her."

"How can you be so sure she didn't murder my father?"

The Kiss of the Dragon Lady

"Because I was with her."

Stacy sits and considers what he said.

"What were you doing? Working off the clock? How do I know you weren't working together all along?"

"You know better than that. The first time I met your father and Susan Li was in this house when your father tried to set me up as a patsy for a drug heist."

"That might be true, but that doesn't mean you two still couldn't have done it."

"If that's what you really believe, let's get the police over here right now, and I'll tell them where Susan Li is and all about the drugs. What do you say?"

Stacy didn't speak.

"You think you know what, and Susan Li thinks she knows where. And maybe both of you want it all, but there's another person who wants in."

"Who's that?"

"You're looking at him."

"You, why should you get a piece of the pie?"

"Because I know where the pie is."

Stacy sat down in her father's chair.

"My father ruled this house and half of the City politicians with an iron hand only to be seduced and then betrayed by Su-Li."

"Betrayed?"

"Sure, she and her pals in Chinatown were skimming off the top of everything coming across the docks from Hong Kong. Su-Li kept the books, so everything was cool, and nobody was the wiser—at least not until something went wrong."

"And what was that?"

"Somebody got greedy. My guess is that my father

decided to check the books and called Hong Kong and discovered shortages."

"And the last shipment? Anything special about it?"

"He was very nervous, I can tell you that, but I can't say if there was anything, as you say, 'special' about it."

"Okay, Stacy, let's get down to it. What did you find in your father's safe?"

"Safe? What safe is that?"

"Quit being cute. The safe behind that panel," he said, pointing to the wall behind her chair.

"I don't have the combination," she said with a tone of defiance.

"I hope you are lying. I wouldn't want to see you get killed for something you don't know."

At the mention of her own possible mortality, she sat up. Her tone changed from defiant to worried.

"Why would anyone want to kill me?"

"For the same reason they killed your father, they wanted something, and I think it's whatever's in that safe."

"But I'm not lying. I've looked everywhere to find anything written down."

"Aren't there any numbers that would mean something special to him?"

"I tried every combination I could think of—birthdays, special dates, driver's license numbers, everything—but I couldn't open it."

"Think. There must be something. Whoever murdered your father couldn't open it. But you can be damn sure they'll be back with something that can open it..., and neither of us better be here when they do."

Pierce stood up and went to the panel, felt around its edge, and found a hidden latch. He pulled on the panel, and it clicked open revealing a small safe.

The Kiss of the Dragon Lady

"This looks like an antique. How long has it been here?"

"Who knows, probably since the house was built."

"Well, it's a simple enough safe. Shouldn't be too hard to get it open. Do you have any tools around?"

"There might be some in the garage, around behind the house."

"Let's see if there's anything we can use."

"You're welcome to look."

"I'm not letting you out of my sight. You're coming with me," he said, and then grabbed her arm and pulled her from her chair.

He led her to a three-car garage behind the house and entered through an unlocked side door. Marcus Williams's Rolls Royce Silver Cloud and the Mustang convertible were there, but he found nothing he could use to crack the safe.

They returned to the study.

"What the fuck are we going to do now?" Stacy asked.

He noticed that her language had only slightly improved since she left the Haight.

"Well, I can't leave you here to have your name end up on the obit page next to your father's."

"Yeah, the big war hero wouldn't want to share column space with his hippie daughter, now would he."

Pierce stopped. What did she say? War hero? What did Williams tell me the day we met? He was wounded the first day he saw combat, twelve days after Pearl Harbor. The day he met Paul Chow.

Pierce went to the safe, spun the dial twice to the left and stopped at 12, turned it a full turn to the right and stopped at 19, then left and stopped at 41. December 19, 1941. He turned the safe's handle—it didn't open.

"Shit!"

"What's the matter, smart guy, couldn't figure it out?"

"I guess not. Your father told me about how he was wounded and met Paul Chow twelve days after Pearl Harbor, so I tried 12-19-41," Pierce said.

"Well, it was a good guess anyway. I never would have thought of that."

"Let's get out of here while we still have our health," he said.

They left the house and walked to Pierce's car.

"Wait a minute. China is across the dateline, a day ahead of us. Let's try 20 instead of 19," she said and walked back into the house.

Pierce tried the safe again, substituting 20 for 19 in the combination. He turned the handle, and the door opened. He took the contents of the safe out and spread them on the coffee table. Together they sorted through them. The safe contained a copy of Marcus Williams's Will, documents for a Living Trust—both showing Stacy Williams as heir with the exception of $100,000 set aside for Susan Li—Marcus Williams's passport, $5000 in small bills, and a manila envelope with three keys inside.

While still examining the documents, they heard a car pull up outside. Stacy looked through the sheer curtains and saw two men in dark suits and hats get out of a blue Ford Galaxie.

"Quick, out the back," Stacy said.

He gathered up the manila envelope and the cash, leaving the remaining documents on the table and followed her out of the study. They hurried through the kitchen, left through the back, ran to the garage, and went in through the side door just as the two men entered the front of the house.

The Kiss of the Dragon Lady

Pierce looked through a window at the side of the garage but saw no one following them.

"They must be searching the house," he said.

Then he saw one of the men come out of the kitchen door and look around before walking toward the garage. He looked for a lock on the door but didn't find one.

"Get in the Rolls and lie down on the floor in the back," he said.

Stacy did as she was told. He followed her inside the rear seat and locked the car's doors. The rear windows were dark glass, making it impossible to see in from the outside in the dim light of the garage.

"Why don't you ever carry a gun?"

"Shush!"

Pierce raised his head and peeked out the car window. He watched as the man opened the garage's side door and looked around before drawing his gun and entering. The man scanned the garage, then looked inside the Mustang. Satisfied it was empty, he approached the Rolls Royce. He tried to look in but could see nothing through the dark glass. He tried the door handle then walked around the car to the opposite side. As he did so, Pierce unlocked the door and lay crouched on his back on the seat with his feet against the door.

Pierce cursed himself for leaving his .38 where he normally kept it, under his front seat of his car.

The man tried the handle and started to open the door. Pierce kicked as hard as he could, forcing the door open and knocking the gun from the man's hand and sending him sprawling across the garage floor. Pierce scrambled out of the car and dashed for the gun, but the man reached it first.

"Hold it, Pierce. I'd hate to have to shoot an old

partner," the man said as he got to his feet.

"Flaherty?"

"Who were you expecting? The Singing Nun?" Flaherty said.

"You okay? I didn't recognize you. Who's that with you, Delaney?"

"Delaney's out sick. I've got a rookie with me today. You can get out of the car now, Miss Williams," Flaherty said.

Stacy climbed out of the Rolls Royce and straightened her dress. Her French twist was unraveling, letting her hair fall down her back.

"I didn't expect to see you, Officer Flaherty, but thank god you're here. Mr. Pierce thinks whoever murdered my father was trying to rob us but couldn't get into our safe. We thought they might come back and try it again," Stacy said.

Pierce studied Flaherty as Stacy spoke. He could tell Flaherty wasn't buying her story, or at least, that she wasn't telling the whole of it.

"So that's why you ran when we arrived?"

Stacy nodded her head.

Pierce spoke up, "What are you doing down here so far from the City? Still playing the Good Samaritan?"

"The Santa Clara Sheriffs are short on manpower. They asked if we would take over the case since most of the leads are in San Francisco anyway," Flaherty said.

"And what leads are those?"

"You know better than that. No way I can tell you anything. Even if I could, I wouldn't. You should butt out, Pierce, before you get in a fix you can't talk your way out of."

"He's working for me, officer," Stacy said.

"You should know better, both of you. Let's go back to the house," Flaherty said.

They walked around the house to the front where Flaherty's rookie partner was resting against Pierce's Healey with his arms crossed.

"Hey, get off of there," Pierce yelled at the rookie.

"You heard the man! Go wait in the car. I'll be out in a minute," Flaherty said.

The rookie did as he was told. Pierce, Flaherty, and Stacy returned to the study.

Nodding toward the safe, Flaherty asked, "What did you find?"

"Nothing much. Williams's passport, a copy of his Will leaving everything to Miss Williams here, and documents relating to a Trust. Certainly nothing to get killed for," Pierce said.

"So you think it was a robbery gone bad?"

"Sure, why not? That way everybody's off the hook."

"What do you mean by that crack, Pierce?"

"Nothing, nothing at all."

CHAPTER FIFTEEN

After Flaherty and the rookie left, Stacy replaced the copy of the Will, trust documents, and passport in the safe.

"Leave it open," Pierce said, "If someone comes back, there's no reason for them to break it open just to find it empty..., and you need to get back to the City. You'll be safer there. Who else knows where you live?"

"Just my friends in the City and a few college friends, that's all."

"That's too many people. Is there anywhere else you can stay?"

Stacy thought for a moment before nodding her head.

"Yes, I know a place."

"And you'll be safe there?"

"I think so," she said, nodding her head again.

"How will I get hold of you? You got a number?"

"It's not that kind of place. There's no phone. I'll call and leave a message at that bar where you hang out."

Pierce didn't like the idea of Stacy going underground, not knowing god knows where, or how to get hold of her. But he had little choice. She couldn't stay at the house alone, and she couldn't go with him, not with Susan Li around. He thought maybe to put her up at his place, but there she would be too easy to find if anyone was after her.

"I'll go upstairs and change my clothes," she said.

"I'll grab the money from the Rolls. Where did you stash it?"

"Under the front seat," she said.

"I'll give you a ride back to the City. You don't want to leave that red convertible of yours parked on the street. It's too easily recognized, not to mention it might get stolen."

"You mean the Mustang in the garage? That's not mine," Stacy said, running up the staircase, taking two steps at a time. "It belongs to Su-Li."

On the drive back to the City, Pierce tried to piece things together. Just because the Mustang belonged to Susan Li didn't mean that she was driving it the night of the stakeout. Or even if it was the same car, however unlikely that would be given the circumstances. He would have to develop his film to make certain.

And how did Stacy know to call O'Callaghan's to reach him, or how she knew Paul Chow was murdered in Hong Kong. Susan Li could have told her, but that seemed unlikely, and if not Susan Li, then who? He decided to ask her.

"Who told you that you could reach me at O'Callaghan's?"

"Why, you did, of course," she said.

"I don't remember giving you O'Callaghan's number. You called me at the office, remember?"

"Must've been in Golden Gate Park," she said.

He knew that wasn't the case but didn't want to pursue it at the moment.

"Yeah, must have been," he said. "Where did you hear about Paul Chow's death?"

"My father told me. What is this, the fucking third degree? You work for me, remember?"

Her feistiness had returned. He was glad. He liked her that way.

"No reason. Just trying to line up the ducks, that's all," he said.

Stacy reached over and turned on the car radio.

...swings so cool and sways so gently that when she passes, each one she passes goes ah...

"Is this the kind of crap you listen to, Pierce?"

"What's the matter with that? It's Sinatra."

"Sinatra? What's he now? About a hundred years old?"

Stacy reached over and ran the dial to KFRC 610.

...one pill makes you larger, and one pill makes you small, and the ones that mother gives you, don't do anything at all...

"Now that's more like it," Stacy said and began singing along with the music.

...if you go chasing rabbits, and you know you're going to fall, tell 'em a hookah-smoking caterpillar has given you the call...

*...remember what the dormouse said
feed your head, feed your head...*

The Kiss of the Dragon Lady

* * *

"Just because I like 'old blue eyes,' doesn't mean I don't dig the Jefferson Airplane and The Doors, too," Pierce said after the song ended.

"Anyone who says 'dig' is hopelessly lost. Face it, Pierce. You're so..."

"I'm so what?"

"I was going to say 'fucked.' But that's not true. You're okay..., for an old guy," Stacy said.

My god, he thought, I think she just complimented me.

He cautioned her to make sure she wasn't followed and dropped her off on Haight Street near Masonic where she would easily get lost in the crowd of like-dressed flower children in counterculture costume.

He liked Stacy. She had an unpredictability about her. On one side, the one she revealed to the world, she was brash, hip, modern, willing to try anything, but underneath her haughty exterior was still a little girl, a frightened little girl who only wanted to be loved.

She might have grown into a beautiful, accomplished woman if she hadn't been raised as a spoiled little rich girl. She still might become that accomplished woman given a chance. Pierce hoped he could help her along the way if she'd let him.

Pierce headed back to Noe Valley. It was getting late, but he had been in the same underwear for two days. After a shower and a change of clothes, he drove down the Great Highway toward Montara. The late afternoon breeze had come up making small whitecaps along Ocean Beach below the Cliff House, but the summer fog was holding off the coast for the moment.

Pierce stopped for gas at the small grocery store in Linda Mar and picked up eggs, bacon, and orange juice— and more liquor. He thought about buying vodka and tomato juice for Bloody Marys, but decided against it. Although he would've liked to stay in bed with Susan Li all the next morning, he realized a woman like Susan Li deserved his full attention. Unfortunately, he knew he wouldn't have time to give it to her in the morning.

He drove to Montara and parked alongside the beach house as far away from the road as possible to avoid the car being seen. The summer fog had decided to drift in from the ocean and would help to obscure the car further, but he dreaded parking in the thick salt air. He reminded himself to get the salt washed off the car as soon a possible. Nothing could rust a car faster than the salt air. Too much of his money and too much of his life were tied to the little sports car to let that happen.

He went to the door and knocked.

"It's me," he said.

Susan Li opened the door. When he entered, he found that she wasn't alone.

"About time you got here, Pierce," said Sergeant Flaherty.

"I'm sorry, darling. When he knocked, I thought it was you and opened the door," Susan Li said.

"A little late for a social visit, isn't it? I thought you'd still be lurking around the Williams joint." Pierce said.

Flaherty was sitting on the couch with his legs crossed, relaxed, at ease.

"Now ain't this a cozy little band of thieves. Seems my old partner and my new one have hooked up and for more than business. Nice little love nest you two have got here."

"That's none of your business," Pierce said.

"I'm not saying it is. What you two do in the bedroom is your business. Gold dragons, however, are my business."

"Dragons? What dragons?" Susan Li asked.

"Let's not be cute, honey. I worked for Williams, too, remember?" Flaherty said.

"So you want to cut yourself in. And don't call me honey."

"It's obvious he knows what's going on," Pierce said. "How long have you known about the dragons, Flaherty?"

"You still don't get it, do you?"

Flaherty paused, took out a pack of Marlboro cigarettes, lit one, and threw an empty matchbook on the table. He took a deep drag on the Marlboro and let out a long stream of smoke.

"I worked for old man Williams back in the days even before you and I were partners in Chinatown. That's when I met your girlfriend, here. Ain't that right, honey?"

Susan Li became indignant.

"I told you not to call me honey."

"Hey, we're all friends here, ain't we? Maybe I should catch you up to speed, Pierce. When we worked together, me and a couple of the other boys were bagmen for Williams and the Chinatown gamblers. You must've known something wasn't kosher even before you reported your suspicions to the brass downtown. You were always the boy scout."

Flaherty took another drag from his cigarette and flipped the ash into an ashtray on the table next to the sofa.

"Well, Williams stepped in and quashed the whole thing, except the other members of the Commission needed a fall guy, and I'm afraid you won the nomination hands down."

"You're saying everyone on the Commission was on the take?"

"Oh, no, all the Commission wanted was to avoid a scandal, so they didn't look at the allegations too closely. They were happy to be convinced by Williams that it was a one-man job that could be handled internally."

"So I got a drunk's pension and pushed out the door after seventeen years."

"You didn't name names, so you got a good deal. You could have ended up on your ass on the street with nothing or even done a little time."

"Yeah, I've been real lucky. I guess I've got you to thank for getting me into this mess."

"Don't blame me, pal. I warned you to stay clear, remember? I can't figure out why, but it was Williams that wanted you to play the patsy."

"Is reminiscing about the good old days over?" Susan Li said. "So you know about the last shipment. Let's get down to business. You told me you went to the house. What did you find, Flaherty?"

"When I got there, the safe was already open," Flaherty said. "Pierce here and the girl ran off to the garage when they saw us coming. I followed, but they didn't have anything on them,"

"Us?" Susan Li asked.

"I took a rookie along with me just to make everything look up and up. He doesn't know a thing. I told him to wait outside."

"The asshole sat on my fender," Pierce said.

He saw the hint of a smile cross Flaherty's face. What a prick, he thought.

"I saw the papers on the table. Was there anything else

in the safe?" Flaherty asked.

"A couple of grand in cash. Stacy kept it. After all it's hers."

"And that was it? Nothing else?" Susan Li asked.

"That's all, I'm afraid," he answered.

"I think that Williams girl knows more than she's letting on. I'll get her to talk," Flaherty said.

"I grilled her pretty good," Pierce said. "I'm sure she told me everything she knows, which isn't much. She's always known that her father was a smuggler, but she thinks it was just opium."

Pierce nodded to Susan Li.

"She thinks you killed her old man, and I helped you do it. I tried to convince her that wasn't so, but I'm not sure she bought it."

"You know I didn't kill him," Susan Li said.

"I know, darling, but somebody did."

"Turns out the official cause of death is a heart attack," Flaherty said.

"A heart attack? Then why are you on the case?" Pierce asked.

"A heart attack brought on by a severe trauma to the head. Turns out he had a weak heart. Looks like somebody asked him some questions he didn't want to answer. Whoever it was beat him up pretty good before they finished him off."

"Now what?" Susan Li asked.

"I don't care what you say, Pierce. I'm going to talk with that little Williams bitch again. If she knows anything she'll talk. Is she still at the Los Altos house?"

"I doubt it. I told her to go back to the City."

"Do you know where she would go?"

"She wouldn't tell me."

Flaherty snubbed out his cigarette, got up, and went to the door.

"She's a little hippie chick. She's got friends. She won't be hard to find," Flaherty said.

CHAPTER SIXTEEN

"I'm sorry, darling," Susan Li said after Flaherty left. "I couldn't help it. Sergeant Flaherty must have found out that whatever was in the last shipment wasn't just drugs. He could have killed Williams, for all I know."

"Perhaps, but I doubt it. He was always a weasel, but I don't think he's a murderer, at least not intentionally. But he could've got rough and brought on the heart attack," Pierce said.

"I hope he doesn't find Stacy. He can be nasty, believe me. Do you know where she is?"

"No, I don't. It's better that way. If I don't know, I can't tell anyone, now can I?"

"You have no idea where the key is?"

"Stacy looked everywhere, but she wasn't looking for a key, she was looking for the combination to the safe. She didn't find anything."

"How did you get the safe open?"

"I guessed the combination from something Williams said the day we first met. I tried the date he met Paul Chow after being wounded."

"How clever, but what do we do now?"

"We wait."

"Wait? Wait for what?"

"Somebody besides us knows about the gold dragons. And that somebody is looking for them, you can bet on it. Sooner of later whoever it is will come looking for us, or at least for you, figuring you know where the dragons are hidden."

"But we do know where they are. We just have to find a way to get them."

"You *think* you know where they are. We can't be sure until we go there and find this mysterious door and get inside, and from what you said, that would be impossible without the keys."

Susan Li plopped down on the couch and crossed her arms in front of her.

"So, what do you propose? We just sit here waiting to see who shows up?"

"This place is too remote. If I'm going to be a sitting duck, I'd rather it be where I can play on my home field. Get your things. We're leaving."

On the way up the Coast Highway, Pierce stopped again at the store in Linda Mar and used the pay phone.

"Hello, Rene, it's Frank," he said when his ex-wife answered.

"Hello, Frank, I hope you're not calling to tell me the check is going to be late again this month," Rene said.

"Nothing like that. As a matter of fact, I'm flush at the moment, but I need a favor, a big favor," he said.

"What kind of favor?"

"I need you to put someone up for a couple of days."

"And who is this 'someone'?"

"She's a client."

The Kiss of the Dragon Lady

"A client? You mean some bimbo girlfriend?"

"No, no, she's a client that needs to stay out of sight for a few days, that's all."

"What is it? Some sleazy divorce case?"

"Something like that."

"What's a few days?"

"Two, maybe three at most. I can pay you a couple of hundred. You won't be out anything."

Rene thought about it for a moment.

"Okay, I guess that'll be all right. When are you bringing her over?"

"In about an hour. And, Rene, thanks. You're a lifesaver," Pierce said before hanging up.

When Pierce got back in the car, Susan Li asked, "Who'd you call?"

"I had to find a place for you to stay..."

"...I want to stay with you, darling."

"I know. I feel the same way, but that just wouldn't be safe at least not for now. You can see that, can't you?"

"Where are you taking me?"

Pierce smiled.

"You'd never guess, so I'll tell you. I called my ex-wife. You're staying with her until we get this mess straightened out."

"Your ex-wife? Won't that be a little strained? Couldn't you think of anywhere else?"

"You don't need to worry. Rene and I get along fine... if her alimony check arrives on time.

"I told her you were a client that needed somewhere to stay for a few days. She thinks you're going through a divorce, so she's sympathetic. You can play the part, I'm sure."

"So, you lied to your wife?"

"Ex-wife. Being married to a cop is hard enough. Sometimes you bring home the shit you have to deal with every day. Sometimes you have to lie so that shit doesn't rub off on the people you love."

"But maybe if you had been open with her, she would've understood."

"Yeah, maybe..."

Pierce continued up the Great Highway, crossed the Golden Gate Bridge, and drove down into Sausalito. Rene had a small apartment on Princess Street close to the center of town. He was lucky to find a parking spot not far away. He and Susan Li walked up a long, inclined driveway and climbed a flight of stairs.

Although it was evening, Sausalito was crowded with tourists.

Pierce turns to Susan Li.

"You're a beautiful, striking woman, and too easy to recognize, so I want you to keep out of sight until you hear from me."

Rene greeted Pierce and Susan Li at the front door. After Pierce made cursory introductions, he gave Rene two hundred dollars and left the two women to size up each other. He hurried down the stairs and to his car, happy to be out of the uncomfortable situation.

"Please have a seat and make yourself comfortable," Rene said.

Susan Li sat on a red leather love seat opposite a television.

"Please excuse me if I don't take off my sunglasses. I'm quite sensitive to light, you see."

Eurasian, tall, slim, urbane, Susan Li was not what

The Kiss of the Dragon Lady

Rene had expected. On the other hand, Rene Pierce was exactly what Susan Li had expected—five foot four, dark chestnut hair with a touch of gray beginning to show, and pretty.

"So, Frank told me you're going through a divorce? I hope it's not too messy."

"Messy? No, but my husband was..., is rich and influential. He's not real happy about my decision to leave. Frank... er, Mr. Pierce thought he might try to find me and try to change my mind."

By the time Pierce got back to Noe Valley, it was nearly ten o'clock. He parked the car in his garage and walked to O'Callaghan's. Once there, he found the usual midweek crowd of locals, mostly young men in their twenties and early thirties, a few with girlfriends hanging on their arms, all nursing either pints of Guinness or green bottles of Heineken. A few older sots, who had their youth chewed up saving the world from Fascism, kept to themselves at their usual table at the rear.

Pierce caught O'Callaghan's eye and nodded. The bartender came over, placed a glass in front of Pierce, and poured a shot of Jameson. Pierce raised his glass.

"Here's to you old buddy, man's most trusted confidant, the keeper of a public house," he said and threw back the whiskey in one swift gulp.

"Where's your girlfriend, Pierce?" O'Callaghan asked.

"Safely tucked away."

"She's quite striking. Very classy. What's she doing with a broken down gumshoe like you?"

"Slumming, my dear friend, slumming... My glass seems to be empty."

O'Callaghan filled Pierce's glass again, took a second

glass off the backbar, and poured a whiskey for himself.

"Well, Pierce, if you're smart, you'll take good care of the lady. A woman like that doesn't come around every day. You fucked up once, try not to do it again."

Now it was O'Callaghan's turn to toast.

"*Ádh mór.*"

"And good luck to you, too," Pierce said.

The two men clinked glasses to scare away the evil spirits and drank to their toast.

"Mickey, how would you like to be a tourist?"

"A tourist?"

"All you have to do is wear a Hawaiian shirt, and hang a camera around your neck, and take some pictures. I'll lend you mine."

"What if I don't have a shirt covered with flowers?"

"I'll give you one."

"Does this have anything to do with your lady friend?"

"In a manner of speaking."

"Is it dangerous?"

"Not for tourists."

O'Callaghan scratched his chin.

"What would I have to do?"

"Just walk around Chinatown and take pictures. You know, pretend you're a tourist from Two Stumps out to see the sights."

"And that's all?"

"That's all. Simple."

"If it's so easy, why don't you do it yourself?"

"I'll be right there with you, but I'm too well known around Chinatown from back when, know what I mean? I need you to watch my back."

Pierce took another drink of whiskey.

"I'll be square with you, Mickey. There could be some

risk. We've got to be nonchalant. Stroll down Grant Avenue and around Portsmouth Square. Take lots of pictures. But what I'm looking for is in Ross Alley. Do you know it?"

"Yeah, that's the alley with a fortune cookie factory, runs between Washington and Jackson. Right?"

"You got it. What I'm looking for is a plain door, probably painted green with some sort of dragon on it. If we find it, I'll take a snapshot of it along with other snapshots of the street, but we don't want to be obvious. If you think anyone is watching us, we'll forget the picture."

"When do you want to do this?"

"Tomorrow, late morning. We want to look like tourists, after all. Can you get Tommy to watch the bar for a couple of hours?"

"Yeah, I think so."

"I'll come by with the camera tomorrow morning, and I've got an extra Hawaiian shirt that'll fit you. You should wear a hat and sunglasses, too."

"I've got all that, including the shirt."

They finished their drinks. Pierce turned to leave.

"See you in the morning," O'Callaghan said.

"In the morning," Pierce answered as he walked out the door.

Michael Leland O'Callaghan felt like a damn fool as he strolled up Grant Avenue wearing a Panama fedora, aviator style sunglasses, and a red shirt covered in a white flower pattern. The two men sauntered along peering into shop windows at smiling buddhas, bamboo fans, and intricately carved ivory figures. Pierce took his time taking photographs of everything. At California Street, he framed the clock on the bell tower of Old Saint Mary's and snapped the shutter.

O'Callaghan read the inscription surrounding the clock out loud, "Son, Observe the Time and Fly from Evil."

"Sound advice," O'Callaghan said. "How do I let you talk me into crap like this? You've been doing it ever since we were kids."

O'Callaghan laughed to himself thinking of the time when Pierce had the idea of wrapping up BBs with a cap from a cap gun in a piece of cellophane to make tiny bombs that would explode when thrown against hard surfaces.

But it wasn't funny then. Not after Pierce dared me to throw one against the blackboard when Sister Mary Katherine had her back turned as she wrote an arithmetic problem on the blackboard. When the thing went off with a bang, our fourth grade teacher jumped, grabbed her chest, and gasped for breath. I was sure she was having a heart attack and croak right there on the spot.

I damn near got expelled. Probably should've. Luckily, Father Murray interceded on my behalf, so I only got a two-week suspension. I'm sure I got off easily because Father Murray knew Pierce put me up to it. Now here I am at it again. Damn Pierce. If he wasn't my best friend, I would've told him to go to hell.

Pierce and O'Callaghan continued their sightseeing jaunt down Grant Avenue until they reached Washington Street. They crossed the street at the intersection and walked up half of a block and turned into Ross Alley, still snapping pictures.

Ross Alley was crowded with locals and tourists. It didn't take long before Pierce found what he was looking for. The door was dark green, its paint peeling. In its center was a stylized red dragon about six inches tall. The door was locked with a Schlage cylinder lock. A small door ringer button was installed in the doorjamb near the top of the door.

He decided to push the button and heard a faint ringing inside. He waited and pushed the button again. No one came to the door.

Pierce handed the camera to O'Callaghan. He found the key in his pocket, put it in the lock, and turned it. The door opened inward onto a short landing in front of an iron gate held closed with a padlock. Behind the gate a small red light was blinking on a burglar alarm panel, and beyond a stairway led down to a basement. He took the second key and opened the padlock, went inside, and inserted the last key into the panel. The red light turned to green. He found a light switch next to the panel and flipped it on.

"Wait here and pretend you're a tourist," he said to O'Callaghan.

Pierce went down the stairs to a large basement that extended under two or three buildings. The basement was packed with old furniture, beat up suitcases, worn out card tables, an old fourposter bed frame, and dozens of packing crates. He didn't know where to start looking or what he was looking for exactly. He scanned the packing crates hoping to find any telltale sign marked on one of them. Off to the side, a few crates sat covered with an olive drab canvas tarp. Pierce threw back the tarp and found two large wooden crates and a smaller one with rope handles attached to its sides. He tried to lift the smaller crate. It was heavy, but manageable, not more than fifty or sixty pounds at most.

Out in the alley, O'Callaghan had been taking snapshots

when he heard a voice behind him.

"No picture here," the voice said.

O'Callaghan turned around to see a stocky Chinese man.

"No picture," the man said.

"I'm sorry? What did y'all say?"

"You no make picture."

"I'm just here for a couple a days for a dentists' convention and thought I'd get some photographs for my wife back in Dallas. She just loves Chinese things."

O'Callaghan failed to notice a slender man in a dark suit that had come up from behind.

"You give me camera," the short man said.

"That's okay. I don't want no trouble. I'll just go now," O'Callaghan said and turned around and bumped into the man standing behind him.

The short man stepped forward and snatched the camera from O'Callaghan's hand.

"Hey! What is this? That's an expensive camera."

The man flipped open the camera's back and pulled out the roll of film, which he crumpled in his fist before putting it in his jacket pocket.

"We wait for your friend."

"Friend? What friend?"

"We wait."

Pierce struggled up the stairs to the landing, carrying the crate by its handles. He replaced the padlock on the interior iron gate, opened the door to the alley a few inches and checked to see if the coast was clear.

He saw O'Callaghan standing in front of the building opposite the door, his arms hanging at his sides. He looked uncomfortable, but everything appeared to be okay.

Pierce reset the alarm and stepped into the alley with the crate. The alley that had been crowded only minutes before was now nearly empty except for a few tourists. He closed the door behind him and heard the click of the lock's bolt slip into the strike plate in the doorjamb. Then he heard the second click of the hammer of a revolver and felt the barrel in the small of his back.

"You have something no belong to you, Mr. Pierce."

Pierce recognized the voice.

"Hello, Yan-ling. How have you been keeping yourself?"

"You walk or I shoot you and your friend," Yan-ling said.

He gestured with his free hand to the tall man who was now standing next to O'Callaghan. The man shoved O'Callaghan toward Pierce.

"You help carry," Yan-ling told O'Callaghan.

Pierce and O'Callaghan carried the crate between them down Ross Alley to Jackson Street with Yan-Ling and the other man following. Parked at the curb on Jackson was Marcus Williams's Rolls Royce. Yan-Ling opened the trunk.

"Put in," he told Pierce.

Pierce and O'Callaghan lifted the crate into the trunk. Yan-ling closed it. Then he and the other man got into the Rolls and drove away down Jackson Street. Pierce watched the car go across Grant Avenue and Kearney Street until it turned right into Columbus Avenue and disappeared.

CHAPTER SEVENTEEN

"What the hell was that all about, Pierce?" O'Callaghan asked when they got back to the bar.

"Just a hunch that didn't pan out as I planned, I'm afraid."

"Tommy, give us a couple of shots of Jameson," O'Callaghan said.

Tommy O'Callaghan set glasses on the bar and poured the shots, which both his brother and Pierce knocked back.

"Another one," O'Callaghan said. "And another one for Pierce."

Tommy poured two more shots.

"I'll be heading home. See you at ma's for dinner Sunday," Tommy said to his brother before he left.

Pierce said nothing, waiting for the whiskey to settle his friend's nerves and his own.

The two men sat with their drinks without speaking for a while before O'Callaghan finally spoke up.

"While we were over in Chinatown, I got to remembering about how you got me in shit with that BB bomb trick you dreamt up when we were kids. If it hadn't been for Father Murray, I would've got kicked out of school. My old man kicked the crap out me just for getting sent home... Are you laughing, Pierce?"

Remembering that time from their childhood broke the tension.

"I thought that old nun was going to hit her head on the ceiling. Well, she deserved it. We both got the scars to prove it. Her and that damn pointer she always carried. My knuckles still hurt just thinking about it," Pierce said and raised his glass. "Here's to Sister Mary Katherine, may God rest her soul."

Pierce finished his whiskey.

If Pierce's hunch was right, Cao Yan-ling had been waiting for someone to come and open the green door. That meant that he didn't have the keys or the combination to the safe in Williams's study. According to Susan Li, two sets of keys opened the door in Ross Alley. He had the set from the Williams study. Who had the other set? That more or less left Marcia Chow. She could've easily taken them from the office safe. Did she know what they were for? Perhaps, but he doubted it. But someone else, someone who knew about the keys, could have waited in the cottage and killed Marcia Chow to get them.

How about Flaherty? Pierce doubted that, too. Flaherty would've provided muscle, but he wasn't high enough on the food chain to know too much about the intricacies of the smuggling operation.

So where did that leave him? Perhaps with someone high up in one of the Tongs? If that was the case, he was afraid he had hit a dead end. That left only Susan Li. Pierce decided he would have to see the Dragon Lady right away.

He walked down to the end of the bar and picked up the phone from the back bar and dialed Rene's number. She answered right away.

"Tell your house guest to get her things. Then take her to the Seven Seas on Bridgeway and wait inside. Watch for me. I'll be in front in less than a half hour," he said and hung up.

He didn't bother taking O'Callaghan's van. Anyone who was onto him would by now have identified the van as his surveillance vehicle. He walked down Twenty-fourth Street to Noe, crossed at the intersection and waited. He looked up and down the street but didn't see anyone following, so he walked to his apartment building, got his car, and drove out of the garage heading north in the afternoon sunshine. When he pulled away from the curb, he noted a black Dodge Charger pulling into the street up the hill. He turned left on Twenty-fourth and right on Castro Street. He checked his rearview mirrors and didn't see the Charger. He continued up Castro Street, over the hill and across Market Street until Castro merged into Divisadero Street. Checking his mirrors, he thought he saw the Charger, but he wasn't sure. He continued down the Divisadero Street hill to Lombard Street, took a left and followed Lombard until it turned into the approach to the Golden Gate Bridge. At the bridge's tollgate, he saw the Charger at the end of the line of cars behind him as he fished in his pocket for a quarter to pay the toll.

This guy's good, Pierce thought. Let's see how good.

At the north end of the bridge, after taking the Sausalito exit, he turned left into Bunker Road. At the reversible one lane tunnel that led to Fort Barry, the traffic light was red signaling that he couldn't enter as cars were coming from the opposite direction. When the opposing traffic exited and the light turned green, he would have five minutes to get through the less than a half-mile tunnel before traffic again started to come through from the other end. Plenty of time. He turned on his headlights.

He checked his mirror. The Charger was waiting three cars back. The light turned green. Pierce checked the sweep of the second hand on his wristwatch as he started forward. At thirty miles per hour, it would take him about one minute to get through the tunnel. When he emerged at the other end, he checked his watch. Fifty-seven seconds had passed. He pulled to the side of the road to see if the Charger had followed him or had waited for him to return. He saw the two cars that were between him and the Charger exit the tunnel, then the Charger emerged. As it passed, Pierce looked to see the driver, a medium built man in a dark jacket and wearing a brown fedora. Pierce didn't recognize him. The driver didn't look in his direction but continued down the road.

Pierce checked his watch. The Charger wouldn't return right away. The driver would wait to see if Pierce continued on. If not, the Charger would be back in a few minutes.

Pierce sat in his car and kept an eye on his watch. When four minutes and twenty-five seconds had passed, he slammed the Healey into gear, made a tire-screeching U-turn and sped back into the tunnel. He had thirty seconds to make it to the other end before traffic would enter. He punched the Healey up to sixty-five miles per hour in the narrow tunnel. He glanced at his mirror but didn't see anyone following. He reached the other end as an Army Jeep was just about to enter. The Jeep driver slammed on his brakes, and Pierce slipped through as the Jeep driver gave him the international sign showing what the driver thought of him.

Pierce pulled the Healey to the curb in front of the Seven Seas, leaned across the seat, and opened the passenger side door. Susan Li and Rene came out of the restaurant.

"Put your stuff behind the seat and climb in," he told Susan Li.

As she was doing so, Rene went around to the driver's side.

"You're in up to your neck with this one, Frank. Be careful, very careful," Rene said.

"Thanks for the advice."

He waved Rene a kiss as he left the curb and drove north on Bridgeway toward the north end of town. He didn't want to go back the way he came. The driver of the black Charger would most certainly follow into Sausalito trying to find him once he managed to get through the tunnel.

At the end of town, Pierce took the on-ramp to US 101 heading south back across the Golden Gate Bridge to San Francisco. Driving up the Waldo Grade and through the tunnel at the top, he kept one eye on his review mirror but didn't see the Charger. Once he felt that they weren't being followed, Pierce told Susan Li about finding the keys in Williams's safe.

She was upset.

"Why didn't you say so before?"

"I didn't want to say anything in front of Flaherty, and I wasn't sure I'd find anything in Ross Alley anyway. For all I knew, it could be a wild goose chase," he said.

On the drive back to the City, Pierce told Susan Li that he found the door in Ross Alley, and that he had a run in with two men who seemed to be guarding it. She didn't seem surprised that the location was being watched. He didn't tell her about the crate or Yan-ling.

"Do you have any idea how the dragons are packed, or what the shipping crate looks like?" he asked.

"It would be a heavy packing crate, probably wood or maybe cardboard. Each dragon stands about twelve inches high. They are heavy, but the crate wouldn't be too hard to carry."

Pierce drove without saying anything for a while.

Then finally he asked, "Do you know where Yan-ling is?"

"Should I?"

"Stacy dismissed all the servants. Would you have any idea where Yan-ling would go?"

"He lived in the servant quarters at the rear of the house. I don't think he had any family, none living outside of China, anyway."

"How did he become Williams's butler?"

"Not only the butler, he was the chauffeur, the majordomo, and Marcus's bodyguard... He took care of anything that needed to be attended to."

"Anything?"

"And everything."

"So you think he knew about Ross Alley?"

"I would be surprised if he didn't. He and Marcus were close. They met in China during the war. After the war, Yan-ling made his way to Hong Kong. Then he came to America about nine or ten years ago. Marcus sponsored him."

The Golden Gate Bridge was already encased in early evening fog when they crossed. At the bridge toll plaza,

Pierce stopped at the tollbooth and fished in his pocket for another quarter for the bridge toll, but couldn't find one. He gave the toll taker a dollar and took his change.

As he drove away from the toll booth, he spotted the black Charger in his mirror. He darted across two lanes and took the Park Presidio exit on his right. At a red light at California Street, he turned right, made a quick U-turn, drove back across Park Presidio as the light changed, and headed east. Although the driver of the Charger knew where Pierce lived, and more than likely saw Susan Li in the car, that was no reason to let the guy tail him.

"Well, it looks like we're right back where we started," Pierce said. "Let's have a nice quiet supper, get a good night's sleep, and tackle everything new in the morning."

"Sleep?" she asked, putting her hand on his thigh.

After a few minutes, she asked, "Did we shake the car that was following us?"

"You saw it, too?"

"I saw you checking the rearview mirror every five seconds and driving like a madman. Did we lose him?"

"I think so. Do you know anyone who drives a black, late model Dodge Charger?"

"No, I don't think so," she said.

"Well, we can't go to my place. Whoever it is, he knows where I live. I know a quiet little inn in North Beach where we can stay that'll be safe for the night."

Pierce drove east on California Street. He turned left in front of the Fairmont Hotel on Mason Street and continued down the hill. He turned right on Vallejo and parked in the Vallejo Street Garage.

"Let's have dinner at The Shadows just like old times," she said.

"Just like old times, a whole week ago?"

The Kiss of the Dragon Lady

"That first night we were together, I'll remember it forever," she said in a sultry whisper.

Their first night, the thought of it sent chills up his spine and stirrings in his groin.

"If I remember, in the morning you were gone, leaving me in bed all alone."

"But I couldn't stop thinking about you. I had to see you again."

After parking the car, they walked down Stockton Street to Columbus Avenue and hailed a taxi.

"This is going to be fun," she said as she slid into its back seat. She sat close, leaned against him, and squeezed his arm.

The taxi took them up Union Street to Montgomery and left them out in front of the restaurant. Pierce kept his eyes peeled. No one was following them.

Inside the restaurant, Pierce made reservations with the *maître d'* at the door. They then climbed the stairs to the bar. The bar was crowded. They made their way through the people to the far end where they stood waiting. Susan Li waved her hand and caught Sam's attention.

"I don't see either of you for months on end, now twice in a week. What can I get you?"

"A Beefeater Gibson and a Jameson on the rocks," Pierce said.

"Of course," Sam said.

While he was making the drinks, the phone behind the bar rang. Sam picked it up.

"Okay," he said and turned to a couple sitting at the bar in front of Pierce and Susan Li. "Your table is ready downstairs," he told them.

The couple took their cocktails, got up, and left. Pierce

and Susan Li took their seats at the bar.

"If I wasn't so hungry, we could skip dinner," she said. "But I'd just get too hungry later if we don't eat now. You wouldn't want me to get hunger pangs later, now would you?"

"That depends on what you'd crave."

She gave him a winsome smile as Sam placed their drinks on the bar.

"Staying for dinner? I can put these on the tab if you like."

"That'll be fine, Sam," Pierce said.

Susan Li raised her glass.

"To health, wealth, and long life," she said.

"And love. Don't forget love," he said.

She smiled and took a sip from her glass.

"And to love," she said.

CHAPTER EIGHTEEN

Pierce put his knife and fork on his plate after finishing his Wiener Schnitzel and picked up his glass of Riesling. He looked into the bright green eyes across the table and felt the familiar pang of desire. She looked up and smiled. He wanted her more now than ever before.

"Let's not go to a hotel. We can go to my place," she said.

"Your place?"

"You know, where we first made love."

"I thought that was Marcia Chow's cottage."

"I used to let her stay there from time to time."

"It's a crime scene. It'll be cordoned off. Besides, you know what happened..."

"The police released the property. It's all been cleaned from top to bottom. Besides, no one knows I own it. It's the last place anyone would think to look for us. You're not squeamish, are you?"

"That's not it. It's just..."

Outside the restaurant, Susan Li hooked her arm in his, and they crossed the street to the Filbert Steps.

He wondered how she knew the cottage had been

cleaned, and it was unusual for a crime scene to be released so quickly. He thought better than to ask her about such things at the moment.

Although it was after dark, Alice Blount was outside on the Filbert Steps. When she saw Susan Li in the pale light of a street lamp, she let out a gasp, and grabbed her throat as if she had seen a ghost. She had.

"Ms. Chow!"

"Good evening, Alice," Susan Li said.

"I..., I thought you were..., they said you were...," is all Alice Blount could manage to get out.

"It was all a mistake, a tragic mistake," Susan Li said. "I let my friend stay here for a while. According to the police investigation report, she must've surprised a burglar. I can't think of any other reason why anyone would want to do her any harm. She was such a sweet girl."

"I just assumed it was you they found. I never looked at..."

"I feel awful about my friend, but I guess I should consider myself lucky. I could've been home when..., Well, I don't really want to talk about it. Good evening, Alice."

Pierce nodded to Alice Blount, and they continued on to the cottage. At the front door, Susan Li dug in a nearby potted Geranium with her finger and found the key to the cottage.

Once inside, she turned and pinned him against the door. Their lips parted. She kissed him. He held her close. She was still wearing the green turtleneck. He pulled it over her head and dropped it on the floor. She wasn't wearing a bra. He kissed her lips, her neck, her breasts. She unbuttoned his shirt and pulled it open, exposing his

The Kiss of the Dragon Lady

bare chest. She pressed against him.

"Take me to bed," she said.

Pierce didn't fall asleep until well after four o'clock. He and Susan Li had made love for several hours before she untangled herself from his arms, rolled over, and fell asleep. Her breathing became rhythmic. He wondered how she could sleep so soundly after all that had happened, was still happening. He felt for his gun under his pillow.

In the morning, she was gone. He wasn't surprised. He was expecting it. He got out of bed and checked the clock on the nightstand: 8:38. He wanted to take a shower, but he didn't want to risk it, and he didn't want to wash away her scent.

He took his gun to the bathroom, splashed water on his face and ran his wet hands through his hair. He looked at his reflection in the mirror over the sink. He was tired. Back in the bedroom, he waited to dress before checking his pockets. The keys to the door in Ross Alley were gone. Again, he was not surprised.

He found his jacket on the couch where he had thrown it in his haste to follow Susan Li up the circular stairs to the bedroom. In the kitchen, he stared for a moment at the place where he had found Marcia Chow's body, or was it Susan Li's body? He couldn't be sure what her name was. It didn't matter now. Marcus Williams and Marcia Chow were dead, murdered, and that did matter. It mattered a whole lot. Pierce was in love with the murderer.

The sun was already high over the East Bay hills when Pierce walked down Union Street and turned left on Stockton. At Vallejo, he crossed Columbus Avenue and

155

picked up his car from the garage. He didn't bother to check to see if anyone was following him. Whoever was in the black Charger wanted Susan Li, not him, and she was long gone, and so were the gold dragons.

At home, after his second cup of coffee, Pierce went to the bathroom and started to undress. When he opened his shirt, his nostrils filled with the scent of Susan Li's intoxicating perfume mixed with the musty odor of stale sex. He turned on the shower, and let it warm up. His mind reached back to the night before. She had left him with a night to remember, for that he would be forever grateful. Smart, beautiful, talented, and the best lover he ever had, or would ever have, how could she love a "poor, but Irish" ex-cop. But he had hoped she had. He wanted it to be real.

Pierce ripped off his shirt and threw it into the dirty clothes hamper and finished undressing.

"Fuck her," he said out loud and stepped in the shower under the steaming hot water.

After his shower and a shave, he got dressed and lay on the sofa and tried to fall asleep. He felt exhausted, but sleep wouldn't come. His mind kept retracing the events that had lead him to..., to nowhere.

He finally nodded off only to be woken by the sound of the downstairs buzzer. He staggered to his feet and went to the hallway and pushed the intercom button.

"Who is it," he asked.

"Inspector Delaney, open up."

Pierce buzzed him in, opened the apartment door and watched as Delaney appeared at the top of the stairs.

"My guess this isn't a social call," Pierce said when Delaney reached the apartment door.

The Kiss of the Dragon Lady

"Can we go inside?" Delaney asked.

"Sure, come on in."

Delaney followed Pierce into the front room.

"Make yourself at home," Pierce said gesturing toward the sofa. "How about a drink? I was just about to have one."

"If you're buying, why not."

Pierce went into the kitchen and returned with a half-full bottle of Jameson and two glasses and set them on the coffee table. He poured a stiff shot in each glass and handed one to Delaney.

Pierce raised his glass.

"'May the wind be always at your back' and all the rest of the bullshit," he said and threw back the whiskey.

Delaney took a sip from his glass and put it back on the table.

"Well, what's on your mind, Delaney? Or did you just miss my company?"

"What happened to your girlfriend?"

"The Dragon Lady? She spread her dragon wings and flew away."

"You wouldn't know where she flew away to by any chance?"

"Not a clue. That joint up on Telegraph Hill where we found Marcia Chow...,"

"You mean where you found her."

"...It turns out it belongs to Susan Li. At least that's what she told me. You might want to check that out, but I doubt you'd find her there or any place else for that matter."

"It's a dead end. Turns out the cottage is owned by a Hong Kong bank. Hell would freeze over before we would get anything from them."

"I heard you guys said Marcia Chow was surprised by a burglar. You buying that, Delaney?"

"I do what I'm told. You know the score. You used to swim in the same water."

"Yeah, I know the score. I played by the rules and got my head handed to me on a platter."

"That's what I heard."

"You got any leads on who did the Chow girl?" Pierce asked.

"Off the record?"

"Off the record."

"We got nothing. We went over the place with a fine tooth comb. Nothing. Not a print, not a hair, nothing. The place had been cleaned from top to bottom. Even the bed upstairs had clean new sheets."

"That sounds like a pro. How about the gun under the body?"

"It turns out that it wasn't even the murder weapon. The killer must've had two guns and dropped one. Nothing on file about it. We even checked with the Feds. The gun had an older serial number. Maybe it was never registered. Or the records got lost. Who knows, the Department was pretty sloppy about such things in the old days."

"Yeah, pretty sloppy," Pierce said.

"You thinking what I'm thinking?"

"We still off the record?"

"Still off the record."

"It could be a cop's second weapon. A throwaway piece if ever needed in a pinch."

"What are you suggesting, Pierce?"

"I'm not suggesting anything. Just that you say there's no record of the .38, which is improbable unless the record was removed from the files."

"How'd you know it was a .38?"

"I was there, remember? I saw it when the crime scene guy showed it to you."

"Yeah, that's right. I forgot, sorry."

"Don't worry about it. No harm, no foul."

Delaney took another drink of Jameson, more than a sip this time. Pierce poured himself another round and filled Delaney's glass.

"I'm sorry, but I got to ask you. Where were you at three o'clock this morning?"

"Who's dead?"

"Don't be such a wise guy. Where were you?"

Pierce smiled.

"The same place I was the last time you asked me that question. As a matter of fact, with the same woman. So, who's dead?"

"Kevin Flaherty."

Pierce didn't say anything. He picked up his whiskey and took a drink.

"How?" he asked.

"His body was found around three-thirty this morning. The strange thing is that he had been garroted. That's a form of execution used by the Mafia."

"Or a Triad. Who found the body?"

"A Chinaman. He found Flaherty on his way into work and called us right away."

"Where?"

"In Chinatown. In front of a cookie factory."

"In Ross Alley?"

"Yeah, that's the one. How'd you know?"

"Just a guess. It's the only cookie factory in Chinatown that I remember."

CHAPTER NINETEEN

The evening was still early. Gray fingers of fog crept over Twin Peaks and were streaming down its slopes toward Noe Valley when Pierce entered O'Callaghan's. Most of the Friday night crowd of Baby Boomers—young men looking for one night stands and young women looking for Mister Right, but ending up with Mister Wrong—hadn't shown up yet. The regulars of the World War II generation were trying to hold court without success at their usual table at the rear. The current generation wasn't paying any attention. They had their own war.

"You look like shit, Pierce," O'Callaghan said as he poured a shot of Jameson for his friend.

"How fitting. I feel like shit."

Pierce didn't touch his drink.

"You didn't fuck up again, did you?"

"Again?"

"The girl. What happened to the girl?"

"Gone with the summer wind."

"Sorry to hear that. Must've hit you pretty hard. You haven't touched your drink."

The Kiss of the Dragon Lady

"I got an early start today," Pierce said.

As more young men and women came into the bar, O'Callaghan became busy serving customers.

Pierce sat at the bar with his whiskey. He mulled over everything that had happened during the last two days— Yan-ling took the crate from Ross Alley; Susan Li disappeared again with the keys to the green door, which supposedly were not needed any longer; and Flaherty was found strangled in Ross Alley.

Nothing made sense. Nothing fit together. If Susan Li took the keys, that meant that she didn't know that Yan-ling already had the dragons. Were they working together? And Flaherty, what was he doing in Ross Alley at three o'clock in the morning? And who killed him? Not Yan-ling, he had what he was after. And not Susan Li, they had been in bed together when the murder took place.

Pierce didn't want to think about gold dragons or Susan Li any longer. He was tired, bone-tired. All he wanted to do was crawl into his bed and sleep for two days. He drank the rest of his whiskey and waved goodnight to O'Callaghan.

A beautiful evening greeted him as he stepped onto the sidewalk outside of O'Callaghan's. The fog had not found its way down into the valley, leaving the evening air unusually warm.

Several young couples, hand in hand, were strolling up and down Twenty-fourth Street. Seeing them made him feel happy and sad at the same time.

When he got to his apartment, he found the door ajar. He took out his .38 and carefully opened the door. He listened. No sound. He checked the bathroom through the open door on his right. Empty. He searched the rest of the apartment but found no one. He flicked on the table lamp beside the couch. Nothing seemed out of place. Whatever they were looking for, they either found it or it wasn't there to begin with. Everything in his apartment seemed to have been left undisturbed.

He locked all the windows, and double locked the front door with the deadbolt that he rarely used and put the chain lock in its slot, knowing such a lock was useless if anyone truly wanted to gain entrance.

Exhausted, he took off his clothes, throwing them across a straight back chair. Then he put his revolver under his pillow and fell into bed. Within moments he was fast asleep.

Pierce felt the warm sunshine on his face and saw the blue Pacific as gentle waves lapped against the shore. Stinson Beach was deserted. Rene was not there, neither was Susan Li. Even the rugged surfers at the south end of the strand were absent. He was alone.

He woke with a start, reached over hoping to find Susan Li, but the bed was empty. Outside, the sun had not yet risen. The luminescent dial of his alarm clock read nearly five o'clock. He tried to go back to sleep but couldn't. His mind raced, filled with the images of Marcia Chow lying in her own blood, Stacy William's whimsical smile, the red dragon in Ross Alley, and Susan Li's green eyes. Finally, he dropped off into the world between waking and sleeping where one's mind relaxes and the subconscious wanders freely.

Suddenly he was awake. Was the green door a red herring all along? Had he been on a wild goose chase as he had suspected from the beginning? If so, it was a cruel deception—three people dead and no brass ring.

Pierce showered, shaved, dressed, and grabbed a cup of black coffee. He took his car out of the garage—vaguely

The Kiss of the Dragon Lady

reminding himself that he really did have to get it washed —and drove down Twenty-sixth Street, out Army Street, and caught the Bayshore Freeway toward downtown. He made good time. The usual morning traffic was only beginning. Dawn was breaking behind the East Bay hills when he took the Fourth Street off-ramp toward Brannan Street.

He parked in the alley behind the Williams & Chow warehouse and climbed the few steps to the rear loading dock. He found the heavy steel doors open. A warehouseman was moving a large crate with a forklift.

"Is Rossi around?" Pierce asked.

"In the office up front," he answered.

"Thanks."

The office was a small space set off to the side and enclosed with walls covered with beaded wainscoting four feet high then glass for another four feet, so anyone working in the office could keep an eye on the main floor. On the glass of the matching office door, small black lettering read: Williams & Chow, Imports, Ltd.

He saw Guido Rossi at his desk. He rapped lightly on the door, and Rossi looked up. Pierce entered the small space. Rossi's desk was covered with invoices, bills of lading, the morning Chronicle and a copy of Sports Illustrated.

"Good morning, Mr. Rossi, I'd like to ask you a few questions if you have a moment."

"You a cop?"

"Private. My name's Frank Pierce.

"Mr. Williams doesn't..., didn't like anybody snoopin' around."

Guido Rossi didn't seem to recognize him from the morning of the surveillance.

"Yes, I know. That's why he hired me before he passed away. He had arranged a private sale and wanted me to take care of it for him."

"You got any I.D., Pierce?"

Pierce took out his wallet and showed Rossi his Private Investigator's License.

"Old man Williams told me somebody would be coming to pick up the package I'm holding for him, but I expected ya last week," Rossi said.

"I tried to get here sooner, but Mr. Williams's heart attack put everything on hold. But now the buyer is looking for his merchandise. I understand it's already paid for."

"I've worked on the waterfront for more than forty years. I was here during the general strike in '34, so I seen a lot of strange shit come across the docks over the years, but I always kept my nose clean. Mr. Williams was always good to me. So when he told me to give the package to whoever came to get it, I said okay. He's dead, and nobody else has claimed it, so ya must be the fellow."

A safe, hidden under a blanket and a wooden tabletop, sat in the corner of the office. Rossi got up from his chair, threw back the blanket, and opened the safe. He took out a package wrapped in brown shipping paper and tied in heavy sisal twine. Rossi lifted the package with effort and dropped it on his desk with a thud.

"Here ya go," Rossi said. "Glad to get rid of it. Must be valuable to somebody, but that safe ya could open with a can opener."

Pierce thanked Rossi, shook his hand, and picked up the package. It was heavy. Rossi was a big, strong man and had struggled with it. Pierce carried the package to his car and stored it in the Healey's trunk. Now that he had it, he wondered what was he going to do with it.

Whoever had been in his apartment, Pierce now knew what they were looking for. Whatever was in the crate Yan-ling took was junk, not six gold dragons. There never were six gold dragons. It had all been a ruse to throw anyone off the trail of the real prize, the package now in the trunk of his car—the Han Dragon.

He remembered how Susan Li looked when she told him about the Han Dragon. Her eyes had had a distant, dreamy quality yet shown as bright as emeralds. He was certain that she had seen it before and not in the window of a secondhand shop in Hong Kong.

Pierce resisted the desire to take the package home, open it, and confirm his suspicion. But he had to get rid of it and fast. His first thought was to leave it with O'Callaghan, but he dismissed that idea immediately. Doing so would be too obvious and too risky for his friend. Maybe at Rene's, he thought, but again dismissed the idea as too risky for her. Susan Li knew that his ex-wife lived in Sausalito. No, he would have to do better than that.

Maybe, hiding it in plain sight, he thought. I'll simply set it on my desk in my office. It would make a great paperweight if only I had papers that needed to be kept from blowing away. How about a locker at the Bus Station on Seventh Street? No good, too cliché. Besides, I'd have to hide the key, I couldn't keep it on me. Same with a safe deposit box.

Pierce drove to Noe Valley and parked in front of O'Callaghan's. He grunted as he lifted the package from the front of his car, carried it inside, and set it on the top

H.L. Slater

of the bar. The regular morning drivers had already thrown back their shots with a short beer and were on the road. The place was empty.

"What've you got there, Pierce? It's not my birthday for another two months," O'Callaghan said.

"I'm sure this is what all the hullabaloo is about. Can I leave it behind the bar for a few hours? I've got something to do."

"Yeah, okay. But's what wrong with your office upstairs or your apartment?"

"I need somebody to keep an eye on it for me. I don't want to leave it unattended."

"Okay, but don't leave it here long. I've already got one bullet hole in the place. I don't need any more."

After Pierce left O'Callaghan's, he drove to the Haight-Ashbury and parked on Cole Street around the corner from Stacy Williams's apartment. He rang her bell and waited. He rang again. He heard the door click open. The door was connected to an old-fashioned door lever at the top of the long staircase, which he hadn't noticed on his first visit. He stepped inside and heard a familiar husky voice.

"What'd ya want?"

He looked to the top of the stairs. The girl standing there was not what he was expecting. She stood no more than five feet tall with jet-black hair, cut short, framing her pale white face. Her thin white cotton shift was nearly transparent in the light from the skylight above her. She was slim, petite, and beautiful. Angelic was the word that sprang to Pierce's mind.

"I'm Pierce. We spoke on the phone."

"Yeah, so what'd ya want?" asked the husky voice that

166

belied the beauty.

"Is Stacy here?"

"Why'd ya want to know?"

"She hired me, remember? I'm the private investigator."

"So?"

"If she's here, I need to speak to her."

"She ain't here. I don't know where she's run off to. Probably shackin' up with her fuckin' guru somewhere."

"She was supposed to call me, but I haven't heard from her," he said.

The husky voice became deeper but softer. She was a panther setting to strike.

"She said you're real cute for a guy old enough to be my old man. Why don't you come upstairs? I just baked some brownies," the girl said.

"So, you think Stacy's okay?"

"That chick is always okay. Know what I mean?"

"If you hear from her, tell her to call me. It's important."

"Okay. You sure you don't wanna come upstairs? Stacy told me about your problem. I'm sure I can fix it for you."

"Perhaps another time," he said.

Pierce returned to O'Callaghan's to pick up the package. He didn't know what he was going to do with it, but he couldn't leave it with O'Callaghan. He found a place to park across the street from the bar. As soon as he entered, O'Callaghan waved him over.

"She called," O'Callaghan said.

Excitement stirred in Pierce's chest.

"She leave a number?"

"I'll get it," O'Callaghan said and went to the other end of the bar. He ripped a piece of paper from a notepad, walked back, and gave the paper to Pierce.

Pierce recognized the number. It was the same one Stacy Williams had given him for the house in Los Altos Hills.

CHAPTER TWENTY

"Let me use your phone," Pierce said.

"Sure, you know where it is. I don't know why you bother to ask anymore," O'Callaghan said. "You want a drink?"

"Let me take care of this first. Then we'll see."

Pierce went to the far end of the bar, picked up the phone, and dialed the number O'Callaghan had given him. Susan Li answered on the first ring. Her voice was low, questioning.

"Hello?"

"It's me."

"Oh, darling, I've been so anxious waiting for you to call. I was afraid something had happened to you. You weren't there when I went back to the cottage."

"I had things to do."

"I called your apartment and your office. I was frantic."

"But you remembered to call O'Callaghan's."

"I had forgotten about the bar. I'm glad I remembered."

"So, where are you?"

"I'm at the house in Los Altos. I didn't know where else to go. I was afraid to stay at the cottage alone. I'm so frightened. Will you... Will you come and get me?"

"Are you okay?"

"I miss you."

"Sure, I'll be down as soon as I can."

"Hurry..., I love you."

Of course you do, he thought.

"Love you, too," he managed to say.

After he hung up the phone, O'Callaghan asked, "Are you ready for that drink?"

"Make it a double," Pierce said.

The traffic on El Camino Real was lighter than usual, but Pierce drove well under the speed limit. He wasn't eager to find out what was waiting for him in Los Altos. So far, the Williams house had been bad luck. Maybe the fourth time would be the charm—or kill him, he thought.

He drove up into the hills toward the Williams estate. When he left O'Callaghan's, he had stowed the package under a blanket behind the passenger's seat and put his .38 back under the seat. He parked the Austin-Healey at the far end of the circular driveway. As he approached the house, he wondered if the Rolls Royce had found its way back to the barn like a faithful old horse.

At the front door, he didn't bother knocking. Inside, he crossed the marble floor to the heavy doors to the study. The doors were open. Susan Li was sitting in the chair that had been occupied by Marcus Williams when they first met and by Williams's daughter later. The chair was a throne for whoever was the current master of the house, and by extension, Williams & Chow, Import-Export, Ltd.

Susan Li stood up the moment he appeared, ran to him, and threw her arms around his waist. She wore a clinging black sheath that outlined the curves of her body. Her

The Kiss of the Dragon Lady

black hair was down, her lips blood red. Her lilac perfume filled his senses. She was wearing her dark glasses.

"Oh, darling, I'm so glad you're here," she said. "I was beside myself worrying about you."

"You got anything to drink?" Pierce asked.

She stepped away.

"I'll get you one, darling. Scotch all right? I'm afraid we don't keep Jameson on hand."

"That'll be fine..., Yan-ling not around?"

"Stacy dismissed all the servants, remember?"

"I thought he might've shown up."

Susan Li went to the liquor cabinet, carved in dark mahogany, which sat to the left of one of the two high windows standing on either side of the fireplace. She took out a bottle of Ballantine's and poured a double shot into a crystal old-fashioned glass.

Pierce sat down.

"One whiskey, no ice," she said as she handed the scotch to Pierce before returning to her throne.

Pierce took but a sip from his drink, put the glass down on the table beside him, and settled back in the chair.

"I've got it," he said.

She straightened herself and crossed her legs, bringing her dress up to the middle of her thighs.

"It?"

"Let's not be coy, my love," he said. "There were never six gold dragons, only one. The one that you've been after all along, the Dragon of the Dowager Empress."

She uncrossed her legs and sat on the edge of her chair, knees tight together, hands folded in her lap.

"That's wonderful, darling. Did you..., did you bring it with you?"

Pierce smiled.

"Now that would've been foolish, don't you think?"

"Where is it, then?"

"You don't have to worry, darling. It's safe.   s"

Susan Li sat back in her chair and crossed her legs again.

God, but she is beautiful, he thought. He wanted to make love to her, right then, right there on the Persian rug.

"Let's get away from here," she said. "I know where we can sell it. We can live anywhere in the world we want and never have to worry about money or anything else for the rest of our lives."

"You and me. Anywhere in the world?"

"Yes, just us, together."

"And what about the police? They still want you for the Williams murder and want me as an accomplice. They'll throw out a dragnet that'll include Interpol which includes the British Police in Hong Kong in case you're interested."

"There are places they couldn't·find us."

"Yeah, behind the Iron Curtain or some Third World country without running water and indoor plumbing. No thanks."

"But I didn't kill anyone. You have to believe me."

"The strange thing is that I do believe you. But you've got to tell me everything right from the start if I'm going to figure a way to get us out of this."

"Oh, darling, I don't know..."

"Stop it. Do you want to go to the gas chamber or spend the rest of your life in prison? We're running for our lives. Talk to me."

"I need a drink," she said, stood up, and returned to the liquor cabinet.

She filled an old fashioned glass with Smirnoff Vodka and drank half of it, neat. She swallowed hard and took a deep breath.

"Dr. Chow called me from Hong Kong. He told me he had come across a rare object that had once been part of the collection of the Forbidden City. He said that he didn't dare hold on to it and couldn't sell it in Hong Kong without alerting the British and Chinese police, so he had shipped it to Marcus, and it would arrive in San Francisco. That was four weeks ago.

"I had heard a rumor that the Han Dragon had turned up in Hong Kong, and I suspected that was what was in the shipment, but of course he couldn't tell me that on the phone."

"So you weren't sure that the shipment was actually the Han Dragon?" Pierce asked.

"Not until I received another call telling me that Dr. Chow had been found dead in his bath. He had been tortured before he was killed."

"Whoever tortured him must've got what they wanted, or else they wouldn't have killed him."

"That's what I thought, too."

"But that still doesn't confirm that it is the Han Dragon," he said.

"But what else could it be? People don't torture and kill unless the stakes are high, very high."

"True enough, but how did I get involved?"

"I didn't know that he had called you. I always made all the telephone calls for him."

"But you said..."

"I lied, I'm sorry. But I tried to pay you off and get you out of harm's way when I learned about Dr. Chow."

"You gave me too much money. It might have worked if you would've just given me the money that was promised."

"Perhaps I was too generous, but it's your fault that I fell in love with you," she said.

Pierce took another drink of whiskey.

"So, what about Williams? Who gave him the not so lightly working over?"

"That was Flaherty. He became overzealous when Marcus wouldn't tell him where the shipment was. Finally just before Marcus died, he told Flaherty it was in Ross Alley. Flaherty had used the place before as a drop for drugs, so he knew that the green door was alarmed and guarded."

"And Marcia Chow?"

"That was Flaherty, too. He figured that she had taken the keys to the green door from the office safe. He knew that was where the keys were kept."

"But you had them all along."

Susan Li didn't say anything but looked down at her lap.

"Who cleaned up the place? I don't figure it was Flaherty," he said.

"I did. I had gone to the cottage to warn Marcia. I was afraid what Flaherty might do. But when I got there, she was already lying dead on the floor. You and I had been there with our prints all over the place. I was cleaning the place when you came to the door. After you went away, I left without that noisy Blount woman seeing me."

"And my gun?"

"What about your gun?"

"The gun I left on the nightstand at my place, remember? It was found under Marcia Chow's body."

"I didn't take it, I swear. It must've been Flaherty. When he came to the apartment door, I snuck out like I said. I didn't know who was at the door. Even if I had, I wouldn't have wanted anyone to find me there."

Pierce finished his drink, got up, and poured himself another one.

"And that leaves us with Flaherty. Who did Flaherty? I know it wasn't you. You were with me."

"I'm afraid I must take the blame for the demise of the former Sergeant Flaherty."

Pierce and Susan Li turned to see Benny Quan standing in the doorway to the study. He had a Walther PPK Automatic in his hand. It was pointing at them.

"Good evening, Benny," Pierce said. "I believe you are well acquainted with Ms. Li."

"I told you to steer clear, Pierce, but you never were one to follow good advice," Benny Quan said.

"Put that away, Quan," Susan Li said. "He doesn't have a gun. Do you, Frank?"

"I think I sent it to the cleaners with my other suit," Pierce said.

Benny Quan walked over to Pierce.

"Let's see," Benny Quan said. "Open your jacket."

Pierce did as he was told.

"Higher and let's see the back."

Pierce lifted his jacket and slowly turned all the way around until he was facing Benny Quan again.

"I can see you don't have anything hidden under that dress," Benny Quan said to Susan Li. "Both of you, sit down."

"You don't have to do this, Benny. Frank's got the package."

"That's interesting. I don't suppose you brought it with you. How about it, Pierce?"

"Want to check under my jacket again?"

"If you had been half as smart as you think you are, you could've been on easy street instead of pounding a beat in Chinatown with nothing to show for it. But you couldn't take the money and keep your mouth shut, could you? Not a little fucking choir boy like you."

Benny Quan waved his automatic toward the two wingback chairs.

"I told you two to sit down!"

Pierce and Susan sat down.

Benny Quan checked his watch.

"Waiting for somebody, Benny?" Pierce asked.

"Shut up, Pierce."

"I'm curious. Why'd you kill Flaherty? You know it's dangerous to kill a cop, even a dirty one."

"Flaherty could provide a little muscle when needed and protection from the police poking their noses where they didn't belong, but he was a hardheaded Irishman that horned his way in and then wanted too big of a slice of the pie."

"And his partner, Delaney?"

"He might look the other way sometimes, after all, he worked in Chinatown, but he keeps his nose clean as far as I know."

"That bit about not knowing Susan Li, I knew that was bullshit. You know everyone, and you have your finger on the pulse of everything that goes on in Chinatown. That's why I came to you in the first place. And that crap about not knowing that Marcia Chow had met her maker after referring to her in the past tense, that was careless."

"Maybe, but I didn't think you caught on."

Yan-ling appeared in the doorway from nowhere.

"Come in Mr. Cao. We have been expecting you," Benny Quan said.

The Kiss of the Dragon Lady

Yan-ling looked around the room and entered, his feet gliding across the floor without a sound.

"Good evening, Mr. Pierce. It is so nice to see you again," Yan-ling said.

"Your mastery of the English language has improved dramatically, I see."

"Yes, I'm afraid my meager attempts at Pidgin English had substantial drawbacks. For that I apologize," Yan-ling said.

"No apology needed. Your English is better than my Mission District accent. Where did you go to school?" Pierce asked.

"In the British Public School system in Hong Kong. My instructors were quite adamant about proper syntax."

"Shall we skip the pleasantries?" Benny Quan asked. "Where is the Han Dragon, Pierce?"

"Not so far, not so near."

"You can imagine my displeasure when I found the dragons in the crate were made of cast iron," Yan-ling said.

"I can assure you, at the time I thought you had taken the genuine article."

"Su-Li, did he tell you where he hid it?" Yan-Ling asked.

Susan Li got up and stood beside Pierce's chair.

"He wouldn't tell me."

"I guess that leaves it up to you, Pierce," Benny Quan said.

"I guess it does."

"Out with it, or I'll put a bullet in you," Benny Quan said.

"Please tell them where it is, darling. I don't want anything to happen to you," Susan Li said.

"Don't worry. If they kill me, they'll never find it. And if I tell them, they may well still kill me. Isn't that so, Benny?"

"I'm sure to kill you if you don't talk," Benny Quan said. "But you'll have a lot of pain beforehand."

"I see your point," Pierce said. "Can you get me another drink, darling. My glass seems to be empty."

Susan Li took his empty glass from the table and went to the liquor cabinet. She poured another scotch, returned, and handed it to Pierce.

Pierce thanked her and said, "Let's cut a deal. I'll give you the Han Dragon, and you let me and her live out the rest of our years in peace and quiet."

"That sounds like an equitable solution," Yan-ling said. "What do you think, Mr. Quan?"

"What'll keep you from calling the cops the moment we leave?"

"Why would we call the cops? We have a murder rap hanging over our heads," Pierce said.

Benny Quan thought for a moment.

"Okay, we got a deal. Where's the dragon?"

"Not so fast. First let's put the guns away. They have a tendency to go off without warning."

Benny Quan put the Walther in a holster at the small of his back.

"Okay, where is it?"

"Behind the front seat of my car out front."

"You mean it's been here all along? You son-of-a-bitch," Benny Quan said. "Yan-ling, go get it."

Pierce got to his feet, his drink in his hand.

Yan-ling left the study and returned moments later carrying the brown paper covered package. As he was setting it on the table next to Pierce's chair, everyone huddled around, eager to examine their prize.

Pierce raised his glass.

"Here's to gold dragons and things that might have been," he said and dropped the glass.

Benny Quan instinctively jumped back to avoid the spilt whiskey. Pierce grabbed him around the arms and chest so he couldn't move, then gave him a quick karate chop at his neck, reached under Benny Quan's jacket, and pulled his Walther out of its holster. Pierce pushed Benny Quan away. He stumbled across the table, upsetting it, and the package fell to the floor.

When Pierce made his move, Yan-ling was still fumbling with the package and didn't have time to react. When he looked up, he saw the Walther pointed at his chest.

CHAPTER TWENTY-ONE

It was over almost before it began. Susan Li stood watching the whole scene play out in slow motion. She had been looking at the package, her heart in her throat, when Benny Quan crashed across the table to the floor. She looked up and saw Pierce holding the gun.

"Oh, darling!" she said.

Benny Quan struggled to his feet and smoothed out his jacket. He stood up straight with his pride bruised more than any serious damage.

"We had a deal, Pierce," he said.

"Sure, sure. But let's see exactly what we have here. Nobody wants to buy a pig in a poke."

"Quite right. That would never do," Yan-ling said.

After Yan-ling put the table upright and replaced the package, Pierce reached in his pocket and withdrew a worn Swiss Army knife with which to cut the sisal twine. After doing so, he closed the blade on the knife and took a few steps back. Susan Li stood beside him and took his arm. Benny Quan and Yan-ling ripped the brown paper exposing an unmarked cardboard box.

They could barely contain their excitement as Benny

The Kiss of the Dragon Lady

Quan opened the box. It was filled with shredded newspaper with Chinese lettering. He dug into the paper and withdrew a cast iron dragon. He dug deeper and found another object, another dragon that proved to be a twin of the first.

"Where is it, Pierce? What have you done with it?"

Benny Quan was yelling. Yan-ling had a stoic look on his face. Fate, it seems, had dealt him a severe blow.

"I'm as surprised as you are. That's the package I picked up at the warehouse."

Susan Li squeezed his arm.

Pierce checked his watch.

"I'm not sorry that you'll have to be going," he said. "But I left word that if I wasn't heard from in three hours, send in the cavalry. The police should be arriving any moment."

"I'll kill you, Pierce," Benny Quan said.

"Maybe, but not today. You better hurry along unless you want to explain about your relationship with Flaherty to some of his friends. It would be a shame to get shot trying to escape."

"Good evening, Ms. Li, Mr. Pierce. Until we meet again," Yan-ling said. "Mr. Quan, it's time to leave."

Yan-ling turned and left the study with Benny Quan right behind.

Once they were gone, Pierce picked up the phone and dialed.

"Homicide, McGarrity," said the man at the other end of the line.

"This is Pierce, give me Delaney."

"He ain't here. A man's gotta go home sometime, asshole. Wanna leave a message?"

"Better get him at home. Tell him that Benny Quan and a guy called Cao Yan-ling were involved in the Williams murder. They are probably heading to Chinatown right now to lie low until they can get out of town. Tell him to call me. I'll give him the details."

Pierce gave McGarrity the phone number of the Williams house and hung up.

"I think I need another drink," Susan Li said.

She picked up Pierce's dropped glass and went to the liquor cabinet. She refilled her glass with vodka and Pierce's with scotch. Pierce came up behind her and put his arms around her. She was trembling.

"Don't worry, darling. They won't be back," he said.

She threw her head back and leaned against him, feeling the full pressure of his body against hers. He buried his head in her hair and inhaled her lilac perfume.

"I was so afraid he would shoot you," she said.

"Quan is too smart for that. He knew he couldn't get anything from a dead man."

Susan Li swiveled in his arms to face him. She kissed him with parted lips. His hands grabbed her buttocks and pulled her into him.

"Oh, darling, we're going to be so happy together. We'll have everything we ever wanted," she said.

"Off course. Let's have that drink now."

Susan Li took her glass of vodka, sat in her chair, and crossed her legs as before. She held her statuesque body erect. She looked confident, even defiant. He remembered the warning Benny Quan had given him on the Muni Pier. The Dragon Lady truly is dangerous, he thought.

The phone rang. Pierce picked it up.

"Yeah," he said.

The Kiss of the Dragon Lady

"It's Delaney. I got your message. What's with the two Chinamen?"

"Quan killed Flaherty in the alley, but both of them were in on the Marcus Williams killing. I'm down at the Williams house now. I'll tell you all about it when you get here."

Pierce hung up and grabbed his whiskey.

"So where is it?" he asked.

Susan Li drank from her glass.

"Still in Hong Kong would be my guess," she said.

"Yeah, I figured that might be the case until..."

"Until?"

"Until I put two and two together and came up with five."

"How do you mean?"

"You, Yan-ling, Benny Quan, and Guido Rossi makes five."

"Rossi? What does he have to do with anything?"

"He gave me the package too easily. First, he pretended not to recognize me. He was a bear when he saw my face the night of the stakeout but a pussycat when I came for the pickup. A guy doesn't change like that overnight, especially a guy who worked on the waterfront for so many years."

"That's a nice theory, but I'm afraid it's not true," she said.

"Do you trust him?"

Susan Li didn't say anything. She uncrossed her legs and crossed them again in the opposite direction.

"Suppose what you say was true. Someone treating you nicely isn't much to go on."

"True enough. But you told me that the Mustang belonged to Stacy. I couldn't figure out what she would be doing at the warehouse in the middle of the night. Later, when I found out that it was your car, everything started to fall into place.

"You were there to pick up the package, but you didn't know that Williams had hired me. Rossi never showed. He must've spotted me earlier. Later, when you found out I was watching the place, you tried to buy me off."

"But I already told you. I fell in love with you."

"When? Leaning on the copper bar or over German sausages and wine at dinner?"

"I..., I don't know when it happened. It just did."

"Then you let me think I seduced you to seal the bargain. How could I suspect you after that?"

"I started to fall in love with you when you first came up to me in the Shadows. You had a shy smile on your face like a boy who was caught doing something his mother had warned him against. Then, at dinner, I looked up and found you looking at me with your sad, deep blue eyes. That's when I decided that I wanted you to make love to me."

"And it worked. I did fall for you, hard," he said.

"And now what?"

"And now nothing. I can forgive you for Williams. Flaherty may have beat him senseless, but I'm sure you had a hand in it somehow. Stealing a priceless treasure, who hasn't dreamt of doing that. But Marcia Chow, that I can't overlook."

"Marcia? But what about Marcia? You can't think I had anything to do with that. Flaherty killed her and left your gun to frame you."

"Flaherty wouldn't have any reason to kill her. I doubt he even knew who she was except a girl who worked in your office. No, it wasn't Flaherty that was waiting for her, it was you. I figure she found out about the Han Dragon from her father and your plans to steal it, so you killed her to keep her quiet."

"It wasn't like that. She had taken the files from the office safe. There were incriminating invoices, check receipts, things like that. Nothing about the Han Dragon. When I confronted her about the files, she started screaming, accusing me of having her father killed in Hong Kong. It isn't true. She attacked me like a crazy woman. We struggled, and I shoved her away. She stumbled and hit her head on the kitchen counter. She didn't move. She died instantly. I didn't mean to kill her. It was an accident."

"Even if you didn't mean for her to die, it's still manslaughter. What about my gun?"

"I started to take it out of my purse when she came at me, but I dropped it. After the struggle and she hit her head, I forgot all about it."

"That leaves us with only one question: Where is the Han Dragon?"

"I don't know, darling, I really don't."

Pierce returned to his chair and sat quietly in thought.

"I don't know what you and Rossi have cooked up, but I hope it works. Right now, you better get going before Delaney and his pals show up," he said.

"But darling, aren't you coming with me?"

"Everything in my soul wants to, but you know I can't. If I did, I could never be sure of you. I'd wake up some morning and find you gone. I'd rather end it now. I'll have some bad nights, but I'll survive."

"But we could be so happy together."

"Yes..., that is a lovely thought."

EPILOGUE

The rain started at the end of October and continued into the week before Christmas. It was still coming down hard in the evening as Pierce walked into O'Callaghan's. A few boughs of pine, a holiday wreath on the front door, high enough to cover the bullet hole, and a small Christmas tree at the end of the bar were the only concessions to the season.

The usual Saturday night crowd was there. Inside the bar, little had changed during the more than four months since the Summer of Love. Outside, a new world of protests, riots, and war was replacing the world of the flower children.

O'Callaghan no longer bothered to ask for Pierce's order. He set a glass on the bar and poured the usual double shot of Jameson.

"This one's on the house," O'Callaghan said. "Merry Christmas."

Pierce said nothing. He raised his glass saluting his friend and took a drink.

"Your ex called," O'Callaghan said. "She wants to know when the alimony check is coming. ...Oh, and a postcard came for you."

O'Callaghan reached next to the cash register, picked up the postcard, and handed it to Pierce. He looked at the picture of a serene beach of white sand, palm trees, and the sun balanced on the horizon of an azure sea. He flipped the postcard over. *Pierce,* in a flowing script, and the bar's address were the only writings. There was no message, only a Chinese glyph. The postmark was Rio de Janeiro.

"Beautiful picture. Who's it from?" O'Callaghan asked.

Pierce threw back what remained of his whiskey.

"A Dragon," he said.

Made in the USA
Columbia, SC
22 August 2024

40918610R00104